A
Group
of
One

RACHNA GILMORE

A Group of One

HENRY HOLT AND COMPANY

NEW YORK

Acknowledgments:

Many people have assisted and encouraged me through the writing of this book.

First I'd like to thank Ian for his generous love and support and for cheering me on in spite of (or is it because of?) the fact that he doesn't read fiction. Thanks also to Karen and Robin, for their enthusiasm for this book and for reading it again and again. Their many intelligent (okay, at times, scornful) comments ensured that my characters talk the talk. They continue to inspire me with the comedy-drama of everyday life.

I owe many thanks to my writing group—Karleen Bradford, Jan Andrews, Caroline Parry, and Alice Bartels—who gave me many ideas and never let me take the easy way out. They encouraged me through the good, bad, and ugly times of writing this book and were helpful guides through the labyrinths and false turnings I invariably took before I found the way of this story.

I would also like to thank my agent, Melanie Colbert, for her tact, enthusiasm, and encouragement, and for her generous faith in my work.

Many thanks as well to my editor, Reka Simonsen, for the respectful and insightful way in which she guided the manuscript to its final form.

There are many friends who have supported me generally and specifically through the writing of this book, and I thank them all. They are too numerous to mention, but I must thank Louise Young for her enthusiasm for this book, as well as for our thought-provoking discussions on how to honor the writing and for inspiring me through her own example.

Henry Holt and Company, LLC, *Publishers since 1866*
115 West 18th Street, New York, New York 10011
Henry Holt is a registered trademark of Henry Holt and Company, LLC

Published in Canada by Fitzhenry & Whiteside Ltd.,
195 Allstate Parkway, Markham, Ontario L3R 4T8.
Library of Congress Cataloging-in-Publication Data
Gilmore, Rachna. A group of one / by Rachna Gilmore.
p.   cm.
Summary: Learning from her grandmother that her family was active in
the Quit India movement of 1942, a rebellion against nearly two centuries of
British occupation, gives fifteen-year-old Tara new pride in her heritage, but
she still objects when her teacher implies she is not a "regular Canadian."
1. India—History—Quit India movement, 1942—Juvenile fiction.
[1. India—History—Quit India movement, 1942—Fiction.   2. East Indians—
Canada—Fiction.   3. Prejudices—Fiction.   4. Grandmothers—Fiction.
5. Schools—Fiction.   6. Canada—Fiction.]   I. Title.
PZ7.G43805 Gr 2001   [Fic]—dc21   00-47278
ISBN 0-8050-6475-3 / First Edition—2001 / Designed by Donna Mark
Printed in the United States of America on acid-free paper. ∞
10 9 8 7 6 5 4 3 2 1

For Ian
and Karen and Robin,
with thanks for the love and laughter we share

A
Group
of
One

CHAPTER
1

Lines. Boundaries. When I look, they're everywhere, holding in—and keeping out. Erin and I walk past a brick house with five girls skipping rope in the driveway. Two turn the rope, the others jump in and out—fluid lines, always shifting. Only, who's in, who's out?

Erin nudges me. "What's with you, Tar? Come on, spill. What happened at school?"

"It's that . . . that loser, Tolly."

"Mr. Toller? I thought you liked him."

"Depends on how you define *like*," I say. "I mean, I thought he was an okay teacher, even if he is an awful geek. But . . . know what he said to me today?"

"What?"

"He was trying to set up a welcome banner in differ-ent languages, and he says, *Hey, Tara, kiddo*—you know, that pseudo-cool way he talks?—*hey, kiddo, what's your language?*"

Erin groans. "Oh, great." She knows what's coming next. It's not like it happens often, but she's heard Mom go on about it, and she's one of the few kids who actually understand.

"So I say, *English,* and he says, *No, your mother-tongue,* and I say again, *English,* and then he says—"

"He *didn't* ask you where you're from!"

"Not exactly, but he asked what my heritage is. I mean, why does he single out kids who look different—why doesn't he ask Lesley, or Doug? They have some heritage, too. But, no, it's just me and Chang and Trev."

"So what did you say?"

"Usual stuff. I mean, if he weren't a teacher I'd've told him where to go, but all I said was my parents were originally from India, and I was born here, in Canada. Then he said, *Pity you don't know your language.*"

"You're kidding!"

"No. I'm telling you, I ought to get a medal for self-control. I just looked him in the eye and said, *English is my language.* I mean, what is his need to . . . to classify me, like some botanical specimen? Why should he decide who I am? Of course, afterwards it occurred to me I could've said, *Pity Kate doesn't speak her mother-tongue—Gaelic.*"

Erin grins. "Hey, you should've said you had mixed ancestry—Chinese, French, Native Indian."

I'm starting to feel better. "Yeah, or made up a country and started to babble." I grab Erin's arm. "Oh! I should've told him something like *drop dead* in Hindi and said it meant *welcome.*"

Erin bursts out laughing. "Perfect! Do it, Tara, come on."

4

"Yeah, well, I don't actually know how to say *drop dead* in Hindi."

"Ask your mom."

"As if she'd know. Dad would, though." I grin. "I'll have to—"

As we near my house, Erin stops and sniffs. "Your mother's cooking. Something Indian."

"I can't smell a thing."

"It's definitely Indian. Smells good." She sniffs harder. "I'm getting a trace of *poori*."

I start to laugh. "Stomach."

Erin will eat anything Mom makes, even the stuff Normy won't touch, and Normy's got the biggest appetite in the world. When we first got her as a kitten, Nina called her Tiny, until Mom said, *That's the worst misfit of a name; that cat is simply enormous.* So Tiny graduated to Normy— short for 'Normous.

I can smell it, too. Indian food all right.

When Mom cooks Indian food, no one ever knows how it'll turn out—she's either in one of her crazy happy moods, and she'll gleefully fling together all manner of bizarre ingredients; or she's shiny-eyed and earnest, trying to be the good mother, and she'll cram in everything she thinks is healthy for us. Lately, since she got laid off, she's been cooking a lot of Indian food. The earnest kind.

"Mmm. Smells *really* good," says Erin.

I put my arm around her. "Okay, okay, come and try it." Before all this Tolly stuff happened, I'd planned to bring up Jeff, sort of casually, to see what she thinks. Maybe after she's gorged herself I'll still get the chance.

As we go up my driveway I say, "Hey, Erin, don't say anything about Tolly in front of Mom, okay? You know what she's like."

Erin laughs. "Poor Tolly, he'd really get it!"

"Yeah—lucky for him I'm too old to sic my mommy on him."

I open the door.

It's a maelstrom. The Beatles. Loud. Nina's into them. I hear snatches of Mom singing—no, bellowing—along with tuneless vigor.

"Hi, Mom," I shout. "I'm home."

She's in the kitchen, dancing in front of the stove. In those green leggings she looks like a grasshopper. She's making *pooris* all right. She turns around and waves, her face glowing. I wonder what's up.

Nina has her usual swarm of pestilent friends over, and they're bopping away in the family room. Nina's wearing a denim hat with a huge fake sunflower. Maya's there, too— poor kid, she looks hypnotized by one of Nina's friends, who's in lime green and purple. It's an assault to the eyes.

"Tara-My-Stara! Hi, Erin. Hey, Nina," roars Mom. "Turn that down."

Nina continues to dance, rolling one arm around over the other. God, nobody does that anymore. Except, of course, her geeky little friends, who rush to copy her.

I march into the family room and turn the volume down. Maya comes running to hug me.

"Hey, Tar," wails Nina.

"Mom said to turn it down."

"Ohhh!" Nina glowers. "Come on, guys, let's go to my room." She flounces off with her oh-so-cool friends.

"Go on, Maya." I nudge her. "You go, too."

Ha! That'll teach Nina. She hates Maya tagging along.

"Tara-My-Stara. Darr-ling." Mom's using her extravagant pseudo-Italian accent. "Come and try my splendida *pooris*."

Erin's already sitting at the kitchen table by the bay window, wolfing down *pooris* with Mom's one-pot *bhaji*. She ignores Normy, who stares unwinkingly at her plate.

From Nina's room, the bass pounds.

Mom deftly fishes a *poori* out of the oil, drains it on a paper towel, and kisses me. Her eyes are dancing. Through the archway, I notice the table in the dining room is decked out with the best china and candles. The napkins are even fluted like butterflies—but there are only the usual five places.

"Okay, Mom, what's with all this?"

"Whaddya mean, what's with all this?"

"Come on, Mom. The *pooris*. The dining table. And the big grin on your face."

"It's a surprise, dahling." The posh British accent this time. "We're celebrating."

"Celebrating what?"

"Now, now, just wait." It's her most pompous tone. "All shall be revealed at dinner, with the entire family assembled—I haven't even informed your father yet."

"Come on, Mom, tell." I start to tickle her. "Tell me now."

Mom squeals, "Stop. Not while I'm frying. Okay, okay, pain." She grins. "Guess who got a job?"

"A job? What job? Where?"

Back to the phony Italian accent. "Work first, darr-ling, ask questions afterrr. Prrress me that last *poori*."

I slap the ball of dough in the center of the *poori* press and pull down the handle. "There, happy? Now talk."

Mom slides the *poori* into the oil and says, "It's a short-term writing job. I had the interview Tuesday and I heard today." On with the posh British accent. "Face it, dahling, you have a brilliant mother." She flips the *poori* over as it puffs.

"Modest, too."

"Indeed, another of my many talents." Mom turns off the burner. "There. Come and try it."

I sniff at the one-pot *bhaji*. Nothing too startling—potatoes, okra, some tomatoes, chick-peas; Mom doesn't believe in messing a whole bunch of pots. If it weren't for Gabby, Mom's mother, we wouldn't even know what real Indian food is like. She always cooks everything separately—*dahl*, rice, *chapati*, and two vegetables.

I taste the *bhaji* cautiously. It's actually not bad. I grab a *poori* for myself and dish some *bhaji* for Normy. I can't stand her fixed gaze.

As I join Erin at the kitchen table I ask, "So where's this job, Mom?"

"At a shelter. I'm to do a report outlining the needs of the women using it. And the best part is, I can do the research around Maya's kindergarten time and write at home."

"Hey, great, Mom. Good for you."

"Yeah, congratulations," says Erin, reaching for another *poori*.

"Erin. That's like your fourth. D'you know how greasy that stuff is? It's definitely not good for your skin."

"Oh, Tara, leave her alone. We're celebrating."

"Yeah, Tara." Erin makes a little face. "We're celebrating!"

Mom pats her on the head and she just grins. If anyone else did that she'd freak out.

Wailing in the distance. Then Maya's heavy steps coming down the stairs. *Waaail, thump, thump, thump, waaail!*

"Lovely. Now what?" mutters Mom.

I can tell what. Nina kicked her out.

Waaaail! Jeez. Maya's got powerful lungs.

Mom picks her up. "Oh, sweetheart. What is it?"

Maya buries her face in Mom's shoulder. "Nina," *heave,* "says," *heave,* "I can't plaaay." *Shudder.* "I want," *heave,* "to," *heave,* "play with her."

"But, darling, Nina can't play with you all the time; she's older than you, and she has her big friends over." Mom rocks Maya back and forth. "Never mind. How about I read you one of my stories?"

Oh God, hasn't the kid suffered enough?

Mom's always taking courses—she's tried interior decorating, watercolors, tie-dye, and now children's writing. We don't want to hurt her, but her stories are totally gaggy, full of clunky feminist stuff. Luckily, Maya's instinct for self-preservation kicks in—she shakes her head and wails louder.

Mom pats Maya's back soothingly. "All right, sweetie; you just come and sit with us."

I roll my eyes slightly. I'm three years older than Nina, but apparently that doesn't count. It's not that I mind Maya around, it's just—Nina always gets away with everything.

But then Maya wriggles over onto my lap and gives me her sunrise smile—slow, lighting up the world—and my heart melts. I cuddle her and kiss her firm red cheeks. "Never mind, Me-Oh-Mayo."

Mom asks, "So how was your day, Tar? Anything interesting at school?"

I glance furtively at Erin over Maya's head. Is Mom mellow enough not to freak out?

Nah. Who am I kidding? There's nothing Mom enjoys more than spouting off—if it isn't racism, it's sexism or the deplorable state of education.

"Nothing special," I say. "Same old."

I just haven't got the energy to talk her out of having what she calls her *gentle little word* with Tolly. Mom's like a tornado. And if I don't dive right into her vortex, she gets all self-righteous and disappointed, like her take on life is the only enlightened one.

But I've got a mind of my own. I mean, she's my mother and I love her and everything, but there's *no way* I want to be a carbon copy of her. And I don't want to be whatever Tolly thinks I am, either.

I want to be me.

CHAPTER

2

After Erin goes home, totally stuffed, Mom switches on her cockney accent, "Aw righ', ven. Naow to get all dolled up. 'Ow about 'elping your muvver look smashing, pet?"

"There isn't time for plastic surgery, Mom."

Mom wags her finger at me. "Funny. Just help me pick something to wear."

"Oh, all right!" I heave a mock sigh. It's actually quite fun going through Mom's closet. Occasionally I luck out and get her to pass something on to me.

Mom settles Maya at the kitchen table with a coloring book. "I won't be long, sweetie. You make me the best picture you can, okay?"

Maya nods. "It'll be a *mas*-terpiece." Maya doesn't talk a lot, but she picks up words and gloats over them like jewels.

Upstairs, Mom and I rifle through her closet. It's crammed—Mom never throws out anything. I like to dig around at the back, where her silk saris hang. They're

11

gorgeous but Mom never wears them—too constricting, she says. Of course, she keeps them, on the basis that one day she'll convert them into dresses or curtains. Yeah, right.

I find an old pair of bell-bottoms, hold them against me, sway to the bass thumping from Nina's room.

I wish I were taller, like Mom. I'm a stumpy old five feet three inches, and Nina's already a bit taller, even though I'll never admit it to her. She's so full of herself because everyone says she's gorgeous. She looks just like Mom and Gabby. It's weird, because, if you take their features one by one, nothing's that terrific—thinnish lips, long nose, light-brown eyes—but, put together, they somehow look great.

And Nina's got their lovely skin, too. Gabby's birthplace, Kashmir, is supposedly renowned for beauties—fair-skinned beauties. It's one of Mom's favorite diatribes, right up there with the sexism in India, the suffocating roles of women—how Indians focus so much on skin color. *You know, Tara, if a girl is dark, she's considered ugly, and difficult to marry off! Small bloody wonder the Brits were able to take over!*

My skin's a bit darker than Nina's, more like Dad's, but apart from big eyes and thick hair—thank goodness, it doesn't frizz like Nina's—I'm nothing special. Mom insists I'm beautiful, but she's my mother, what else can she say?

It's not that I care—I'm not a mindless bimbo, endlessly fixating on hair and guys. But it is kind of sickening to have a sister guys might be after more than me. I guess I've been thinking more about it lately because of, well, Jeff. My mind does stray towards him an awful lot—it's alarming. And exhilarating.

"Hey, Tara, where the heck are you?" calls Mom.

"I'm looking, I'm looking." I work my way out with an armful of clothes.

Mom's room is a total wreck by the time I find the dusty-rose chiffon dress she forgot she had.

"Perfect." Mom smiles. "You do have an eye, pet." She looks at the mess of clothes on her bed and floor. "Oh, I'll clean up later."

Dad gets home just as Nina's horde leaves. He makes his way through the gaggle of girls and swings Maya around. "How's my Me-Oh-Mayo?" Maya breaks into her smile and hugs him tight.

He sees Mom. "Wow! Look at you! Are we going somewhere? What did I forget?"

"It's a surprise. Go and change, Raj. The wine is chilling, and I've made a wonderful dinner."

Dad catches her around the waist and gives her a big kiss, right on the mouth.

I moan, "D'you have to do that in front of us?"

Mom grins and calls after Dad as he goes upstairs, "We're eating in five minutes, Raj. Nina, did you hear?"

"Yeah, yeah, I heard." She's still at the door, shouting after her friends.

"Maya, go wash up. Scrub nicely, now, just like I showed you."

"Okay," says Maya. "I'll do it thor-ough-ly."

We don't all sit down until half an hour later. Maya has to be changed, 'cause she got soaking wet washing up *thor-ough-ly*, and the *bhaji* isn't hot enough anyway. Then, because this is an elegant meal, Mom reminds us of the no

BFT rule. That's no *bodily-function talk*, and the reminder is mostly for Nina, who, as soon as we start to eat, invariably disgorges some disgusting story featuring nasal discharge, diarrhea, or vomit, or, if she's feeling particularly refined, ear wax or body odor.

So Nina decides that, if it's an elegant meal, the plain glasses won't do for us, and she insists on taking out crystal tumblers. There's a long argument. Nina pouts and Mom says, "Oh, we are celebrating after all," and I say, "Mom, she's so spoiled," and Mom says, "Please, let's not fight, it is my big day," then Dad says, "Will someone kindly tell me what's going on?" and I say, "I know, I know," and Nina says, "You always tell her everything, you treat me like a baby, I never get to know anything." Then Maya climbs onto her chair and foghorns, "I want my cushion," and that stops us, and we finally sit down to eat.

"Okay, Ro," says Dad. "What's the surprise?"

Mom tells about the job in her usual dramatic fashion—she's big on italics—and there is the expected chorus of exclamations and questions.

There's something strange about Dad. At first, I can't quite put my finger on it. He's quiet, but he always is, so it's not that. More like preoccupied. And a bit restless. I wonder when Mom will notice.

We've almost finished eating when Mom says, "Raj, I thought you'd be *pleased*."

"I am."

"Could have fooled me. I expect a bit of cheer and enthusiasm. It's not every day I land a job."

"Sorry, Ro. I am pleased. Really." Dad wipes his mouth

14

with his napkin. "It's just, it was a busy day and I'm a bit tired. And . . . I have some news, too."

"Not your job!" Mom's voice is sharp. Ever since she lost hers, she's been paranoid about Dad's, even though he's an engineer and one of the top people in his company.

Dad smiles widely. It's a bit fake. "No, no, nothing like that. Actually it's good news. The celebration fits perfectly." He looks around the table. "Mummyji phoned me at the office today."

"Ah. Your Mother. How is she?"

Mom always refers to Dad's mom as *Your Mother*—with capitals.

"Oh, she's fine, fine. Sends her regards to everyone." Dad shifts awkwardly.

Mom looks suddenly wary. Even Nina is quiet.

Dad clears his throat. "You know, she's lonely. One of her close friends died recently and . . ." It's like his eyes are saying *please*. "Anyway, she thought it's been so long, and maybe she, that is, she wondered if we'd go to India for a visit; after all, we haven't been there since before the kids were born, and then I went when Papaji died, but that was years ago, and of course, it's easier for one person—there are so many of us, and she's never been here." Dad runs his fingers through his thinning hair. "So we got talking about her coming, and of course I thought it was a wonderful idea, and, well, girls, your grandmother is coming for a visit."

There is a blank silence.

Maya looks up from the potato she is cutting into tiny pieces and asks, "Gabby's coming?"

We all call her Gabby—apparently, I came up with that when I started to talk, and it stuck.

"No, not Gabby. My mother." He smiles again, a little too hard. "Well, aren't you lucky, girls. You'll get to meet your other grandmother."

Maya says, "Daddy's mommy?"

"Yes, my mother. She's the one who sends you birthday cards from India, sweetie," says Dad.

Nina blurts, "Hey, why's she coming? I thought she didn't like Mom or something."

Oh, great! Leave it to Nina to say something so totally tactful.

"Nina, it's not like that at all," Dad snaps. He turns to Mom. "Rohini. . . ."

Mom looks like she's swallowed a bug. She notices us staring and manages a smile.

"*Of course* she must come, Raj. She is Your Mother." There's a trace of her real British accent, not the exaggerated put-on one—she lived in England for a few years, and it slips out when she's being gracious or controlled.

She tilts her head. "And when might we expect the pleasure?"

Dad turns red and mumbles, "Er, well, a little over three weeks? We, er, thought October would be best, before it gets too cold. And it would be nice if she got to see the fall colors. Of course, it's too bad I used up all my vacation, but I told her, and so, of course, Rohini, if it's all right?"

Mom smiles even more graciously—something I wouldn't have thought humanly possible. "*Of course* it is. Three weeks. Mmm. How nice. How *very* nice."

16

CHAPTER
3

After dinner, Nina and I get suckered into watching Maya as we do the dishes. Mom and Dad disappear into the living room with their coffee, shutting the door firmly behind them. I'd love to be a fly on the wall in there.

I wrap Maya in a huge apron and let her play with the soap bubbles in the sink, while Nina and I clear the table. It's Nina's turn to load the dishwasher. She's subdued and a bit sulky.

I elbow her and say out of the corner of my mouth, "Jeez, was that weird or what?"

Nina grunts. "How come *I* get blamed for everything? What'd I do, anyway?"

I roll my eyes. "What d'you expect? You were hardly tactful."

"Well, what am I supposed to do? Pretend it isn't totally strange? She's never even been here, but we see Gabby and Gampy all the time."

"Well, duhhh! Toronto's just a bit closer than India—"

"But it's not like she's poor or anything. Anyway, Rittie and Bish visit, and they live in B.C., and they're artists, they're hardly rolling in it. But we've never—"

"Hey, relax! Who's disagreeing? And watch it. You're dripping water on the floor."

"Sorry." Nina wipes it up. She looks really down now.

I can't help feeling sorry for her.

"It's okay, Nina. It wasn't just you. I guess Dad's kind of touchy about it."

"No kidding. And Mom! Did you see the way she looked?"

I grin. "Yeah. Like a constipated cow."

Nina giggles and her face slides into a dead ringer for Mom's. I burst out laughing.

Maya turns around, lifting bubbly hands from the sink. "What? What's funny?"

"Nothing," I say hastily. "Look, Maya." I blow the bubbles from her hands. "See if you can make pretty shapes, okay?" I transfer some bubbly water into a bowl and move Maya to the table.

Maya sighs and returns to the bubbles.

I wink at Nina and start washing the crystal glasses.

Nina says in a low tone, "Did Mom ever tell you anything about it—why they don't get along?"

I shake my head slowly as I rinse the glass.

It's funny. The only person we've met in Dad's family is his older brother, Uncle Prakash; but that was when Maya was a baby, and he was only here because of some medical conference. I sort of remember how polite he and Dad were—so different from the way Mom kids around with her sister, Rittie.

We don't know a whole lot about Dad's family, but it's something we've always taken for granted because it's familiar. It's only when I look closely that I see it's like a kaleidoscope—very few pieces, and the rest is just mirrors faking a full pattern.

Pretty much all we know is that Mom and Dad met when they were students at McGill University. Dad had just come from India, but Mom had lived here for years—she was born in India, but Gabby and Gampy moved to England when Mom was thirteen and Rittie was ten, then came here when Mom turned sixteen. Apparently, Dad fell for her big time; only she wasn't interested at first, because she thought he was a typical Indian male—a sexist pig. But eventually she succumbed, and they got married. Afterwards, they went to visit Dad's parents in India, and *that's* when it gets patchy. . . .

I put the glass on the draining board. "Didn't Mom say something about how Dad's family weren't happy about them getting married in Toronto?" I frown and tuck my hair behind my ear. "But—"

"That's a load of bull!" says Nina, shoving cutlery into the dishwasher. "How big a deal is that?"

"Yeah, it's gotta be more than that. I mean . . ." I shake my head. "Dad's so *awkward* when he talks about his family. It's like he's proud but also—shifty."

"*Especially* if Mom's around. And she's always . . ."

Nina's face melts into Mom's gracious one, and we chortle together, "Marmee."

It's what we call those fits of discretion Mom slips into. After Marmee in *Little Women*—the mother who never loses her cool, just presses her lips tightly together when she's pissed off.

I turn to Nina suddenly. "Oh my God, what d'you think they're like if *Mom* doesn't say anything?"

Nina's eyes are round.

"Imagine how *awful* they must be. I mean, the *only* thing I've ever heard her say about them is, *There were some differences.*"

Nina gasps. "Oh! The dowry thing!"

"Don't be silly. Gabby and Gampy don't believe in it, and Mom's never . . ."

"I bet they did, Dad's parents. Bet they expected an arranged marriage, a big dowry—"

"No way, it's not that." I start washing the wooden spoons.

"How do you know?"

"I asked Mom. Ages ago. And she went all indignant and huffy. *Of course not!*"

"How come she tells you and never tells me?" It's Nina's whiny tone.

"'Cause I ask her, dummy. Get drying those glasses, will ya."

Nina makes a face. "Well, if you know so much, how come you don't know why they cut Dad off?"

"They didn't cut him off, stupid."

"Yes, they did—"

"No, they didn't—they still phone each other. I mean, d'you have to be so melodramatic? Real people don't go cutting each other off."

"*Some* do. I bet *some* people—"

"In a soap opera maybe, but not in real life, dummy!"

"You're such a know-it-all!"

"Oh, shut up, Nina. Let's just get this done."

"Fine!" Nina wipes the glasses in offended silence.

"Bubbles, bubbles, bee-you-ti-ful bubbles," sings Maya, lifting her hands and letting the bubbles drop.

I start on the big pot. As usual there are burn marks on the bottom. I bang it around a bit.

Nina glances at me tentatively. "Sorry, Tara." She's crushed again; it makes her look about six.

My anger dissolves. "It's okay, I'm sorry too."

Nina sighs. "It's kinda strange having a grandmother we've never met, isn't it?"

"Yeah." I grin slyly. "But who cares—I mean *she* isn't even a jailbird."

Nina snorts and claps her hands over her mouth.

"No, *her* only claim to fame is she *married* a jailbird."

Nina and I have the worst time not cracking up when Dad talks about it—does he ever get mad! He insists it had to do with the freedom movement, all that stuff with Mahatma Gandhi, fighting the British for Indian Independence and everything, but still. Dad's father was arrested several times in the 1940s, and Dad's grandfather, too; and I think Dad even said something about his mother's relatives being arrested when she was a teenager—I mean, they were in and out of jail like yo-yos.

Nina wags her head from side to side and says softly, in a fake Indian accent, "Oh my goodness, Tara, what do you think our esteemed grandmother sounds like?"

We start to laugh again, look at Maya, and choke it down.

Nina's eyes dance with manic glee. "Wouldn't it be funny if she's really, really Indian?" She starts to sputter. "With big jewelry and nose rings and stuff. You know, like that woman in the latest *National Geographic*? Carrying pots of water on her head."

We're practically rolling on the floor. We know we're being really awful, but that just makes it funnier. I dart a quick look at Maya. She stares at us, then turns disdainfully back to her bubbles. It flashes through my head—what would Tolly think?

I sober up first. "You're awful, Nina. If anyone else said that, it'd be racist. It's a horrible stereotype."

"Oh, lighten up, I'm just kidding." Nina puts on her Indian accent again. "Just joking, oh yes indeedy. Curry and rice, ver-rry, very nice."

"Monster." I grab her around the neck and wrestle.

Maya gapes at us. "Why're you fighting?"

"Oh, we're not fighting, Maya, just . . . just playing."

Nina puts her arm around me and grins.

Maya scowls. "You're not telling." She turns back to her bowl.

Nina nudges me. "Say, are there any pictures of her?"

I grab her arm. "Yes. In Dad's album. I've seen one, ages ago."

"What does she look like?"

"I don't remember. Come on. Maya, we'll be right back."

We race up the stairs to the oak shelf in the hallway where the picture albums are kept. I grab the dusty gray one. Nina crowds me. We giggle as we turn the pages.

"There."

It's an old black-and-white picture with *Mummyji* and *Papaji* written underneath in Dad's writing. It shows a man and a woman standing in front of a tree. The man is tall and the woman well below his shoulder. She's wearing a plain sari, and there don't seem to be nose rings or even any particularly extravagant jewelry. I can't make out her face clearly, but it has a firmness that reminds me of someone—not Dad.

"Oh," says Nina. "Kinda boring, huh?"

I grin. "Yeah, I guess that's the long and short of it." I point at him and whisper, "Jailbird."

Nina collapses against me, laughing. We hug each other.

CHAPTER
4

I tell Erin about the grandmother on the way to school the next morning. She listens in that intense way she has, her green eyes bright.

"I mean, my *grandmother* is coming for a visit, and I don't even know what to call her." I switch my violin to my other hand. It's a drag carrying it, but Hélène, my violin teacher, lives on the way home from school.

"What's your dad call her?"

"Mummyji. The *ji* is a sign of respect, I know that much."

"So how about Grandmotherji?"

"It sounds so weird." I make a face as we cut across the park near our school. "I bet there'll be no nickname like Gabby."

Erin says, "Well, if she's like your Gabby she's going to be all right."

"Yeah, but Gabby . . ." I trail off.

I can't just come out and say it. Gabby, she wears dresses

or pants for everyday, and saris only when she's dressing up, and she's way elegant. Also, she speaks perfect English, just like Gampy.

And, okay, I know Dad's mother isn't like that woman in the *National Geographic*—but what if she is like those old Indian women I see at the grocery stores? They have thin, tightly pulled-back gray hair, and they always wear white, a widow's color, whether it's the baggy pants and tunic or saris. A lot of them walk with an arthritic sway, like crippled crabs wagging sideways. They're so heavy around the hips—heavy accents, heavy hips.

"What?" asks Erin, as we go in the side door and weave through the crowd of kids to our lockers.

I flush. "Nothing."

Erin's eyes gleam. "It's all so interesting, Tar. *Bizaaaarre.* I mean, it's like something out of a book."

"A book, Erin?" I squint at her as I heave my violin into my locker and stretch my cramped fingers.

"Yes. All this mystery." Erin wags her eyebrows and drops her voice. "A skeleton in the closet."

"Well, I'm so glad you find it entertaining. You'll have to come over every day, to see how the soap opera progresses." I pull out my history text.

"Hey, come on, don't spaz. I didn't mean it like that."

A group of guys come down the hallway. Jeff's behind them. He's new, so he doesn't quite fit in yet. His locker is down a bit from mine. As he nears, he smiles tentatively at me. Erin's gabbing on about something as she drags a brush through her short red hair. I don't hear a word she's saying.

"Hi, Tara." Jeff slows down. "How're you doing?"

"Hi. I'm fine."

Jeff nods, flushes slightly, and keeps going.

Great, just great.

He asks how I'm doing and that's all I can say. I thump down my history book. I'm not dumb. I talk to Erin easily enough, to all my friends, and I'm not quiet on the inside—so why can't I find the right words when it counts? *Fine.* Okay, I've never wanted to be part of the in crowd, jabbering away, every other word *like like like*, but just once . . . I bang my head against the locker.

"What's with you?" Erin looks concerned. "Okay, okay, I'm sorry." She yanks out her French grammar, spilling books on the floor.

"It's not that."

Erin looks at me, then down the corridor. "Ooohhh!" She quirks her eyebrow and mouths, "Jeff?"

I'm turning red. I can feel it.

Erin grins. "So—how long has this been going on?"

"Nothing's going on, nothing." I don't mean to sound angry.

"Whatever you say, kiddo." Her smile widens. "Nice, extremely nice—I approve."

"It's nothing, okay?"

"Hey, I saw how he looked at you."

"Did he? D'you think he . . . ?" I can't help it. I break into what I know is a completely idiotic grin.

Erin puts her arm around me. "Yes. Definitely. Hey, how come you never told *me* before? I mean . . ."

Just then the bell goes.

As we shut our lockers, Erin whispers, "I want to hear every single detail."

I don't see her alone again until the end of the day, but I tell her about it as we head home from school. It's such a relief not to keep anything from Erin—I hate being a bubble head, but I do feel a certain elation talking about Jeff.

Jeff isn't gorgeous in a stud kind of way, he's more what you'd call nice-looking. Mostly he's really bright and *not* an egotistical jerk, unlike the dumb jocks a lot of girls seem to go for.

I hadn't noticed him particularly till that loser Brad and his friends were hanging around the lockers going on about how some girl was stacked. Jeff was nearby and he shook his head. Brad saw him and said, "Hey, come on, Jeff, you a priest or something?" And Jeff gave them a look of real contempt and said, "Get a life." Then he happened to look at me and I smiled, and he smiled back. Usually his face is a bit somber, but when he smiles—wow!—it's a flash of light.

Since then, I've noticed him in class, and I like the way he doesn't show off, unlike that brown-nose, Guy, who's always sticking up his hand to impress the teachers. But when Jeff's asked a question, his answer is always worth listening to. Then I started to notice his eyes, this amazing blue, and I think I've caught him looking at me quite a lot.

Erin grins. "I really think he's interested, Tar. Trust me, I see the signs. I'm never wrong."

I almost forget about my violin lesson and walk past Hélène's driveway, until Erin reminds me.

It's probably one of my worst lessons ever—Hélène

never gets mad, but she plaintively asks me to practice more. I smile guiltily. I took up the violin only because Nina started the piano and I wanted a different instrument. Hey, at least I stuck with it—Nina's been through the piano, cello, and trumpet.

My head's still above the clouds as I walk home after the lesson. It's a gorgeous evening, with bursts of red and yellow amongst the green leaves. I drink in the sunshine, and wallow in Erin's words. I replay the few times Jeff and I have talked, the way I've caught him looking at me. . . .

I'm well and truly wrapped in a wonderful Jeff haze.

CHAPTER
5

Then I open the front door.

"... But it's not fair," shrieks Nina.

Clash, bang from the kitchen. "Nina." Dad's voice. "There's no need for histrionics."

Jeff starts to fade like mist.

I catch a glimpse of Nina's face—it's almost round with sulking. Mom is sitting across the table from her; Dad is by the stove, shifting pots with more energy than strictly necessary. It's his night to cook.

Hey, I'm not getting into this. Quietly, I head for the stairs. I wave to Maya, who is in the family room cuddling Normy as she watches *Sesame Street*.

But Mom sees me. "Oh, Tara, come in here, pet, we have something to discuss."

Dad darts a disappointed look at Nina. "Yes, I'm sure Tara is going to be more mature about this."

Huh? Dad hardly ever gets mad at Nina.

I stop under the archway between the hall and the kitchen, trying desperately to hold on to Jeff. "Er, I have a lot of homework, and I should practice my violin. . . ."

"It can wait," says Mom with Marmee-ish determination.

My family. I let out a small sigh as I join them.

Mom says smoothly, "Go ahead, Raj."

What? Usually Mom does the talking.

Dad clears his throat. "Tara, Rohini and I have talked it over and we both agree, don't we?" Dad's smile is the funniest mixture of awkwardness and urgency. I'm starting to get curious.

"We certainly do," says Marmee.

Dad continues, "As you know, Mummyji is coming, and, naturally, we want her to be as comfortable as possible here."

The grandmother. I'd totally forgotten.

Dad shifts in his chair. "But our basement, well, it can be damp this time of year—it's hardly suitable for someone not used to our climate. So we were considering where . . ."

The basement. That's where the spare room is, where Gabby and Gampy and all our visitors stay.

Nina's slumped in her chair, scowling, arms tightly crossed. My stomach goes cold.

Dad clears his throat again. "And we thought the best solution would be for one of you girls to move downstairs. Let Mummyji have your room."

Nina's eyes glitter triumphantly as my mouth falls open.

No way. That spare room's a rat's nest of Mom's abandoned projects; it's stuffed with everything she can't bear to throw out.

"Well, I'm in high school," I say firmly, "and I have tons of homework, so, if anyone has to move, it should be Nina."

Nina gasps. "Why do I always get stuck with everything? Just because I'm the middle—"

"You always say that, Nina, you're so—"

"Girls, that's enough!" Mom's dropped the Marmee tone. "Now, we've agreed, the basement room is out of the question and—"

I interrupt. "Who's agreed? I haven't agreed. Nina hasn't agreed."

Nina nods.

Mom slaps her hand on the table. A glass of water rattles, spilling a few drops. "Look, the basement is *not* suitable for an extended stay, and that's that."

Nina and I look at each other. She's thinking what I'm thinking.

Then Nina clears her throat, and in her polite, controlled voice, an uncanny imitation of Mom's, says, "And may I ask how long Dad's mother will be here?"

Mom's face is a mask.

Dad says awkwardly, "She has an open ticket; that way she can, er, keep it flexible, and of course we hope she'll stay for a few weeks at least; it's such a long way. . . ."

Marmee's smile switches on. "Yes, it's a very long journey for Your Grandmother. It's going to be *very nice* for you girls to meet her, and needless to say, we want to make her as welcome as possible."

My heart starts to pound. She's been upgraded, or is it downgraded, from Dad's mother to *Your Grandmother*. Well, tough. I'm not moving down there for her. And I'm not letting Nina, either—Mom and Dad are trying to divide and conquer. I look straight at Nina and smile grimly. Her face brightens.

For a few seconds, Mom eyes us pleadingly. Then she sags back in her chair and sighs.

Dad rubs the back of her neck. "Rohini, do you think maybe that room will do? I don't think Mummyji will mind, she—"

"Of course it won't do, Raj. Not for *Your Mother*."

I quirk my eyebrow at Nina. Dad's mouth tightens the slightest bit.

Mom says quickly, "Her house is always perfect and you know how particular . . ." She rushes on, defensively, "Of course, she has servants, so it's easy for her, but Indians who come here never understand . . ."

"Dad's mother has servants?" says Nina. "Hey, cool."

I mouth, *Shut up*.

Dad says tightly, "Rohini, she's coming to see us, not the house."

Mom's nostrils flare like she's a warhorse going to battle. "Yes, but the fact is, Raj, for *Your Mother*, the state of the house reflects on *me*, not on *you*."

Dad says angrily, "It's *our* house, both of ours, and—"

"If that isn't just like a man! How convenient of you to forget what she was like when—" She notices us staring, and stops abruptly.

Nina and I exchange glances.

The corners of Mom's mouth come down. "It's just . . .

I'd like this visit to be as . . . as *successful* as possible." Her voice is shaky.

Dad puts his arm around her and looks at us firmly. Oh no. Dad usually vacillates, but when he puts his foot down . . .

"All right, girls, looks like we'll have to toss a coin."

I say quickly, "Wait. Mom, Dad, I think the basement room can work. Just let me finish." It comes to me as I talk. "Why don't we clean it out? You've always wanted to; now's the chance. And I bet it can be really gorgeous if we . . ."—I pause for dramatic effect—". . . *redecorate* it."

A faint gleam comes into Mom's eyes—interior decorating was one of her favorite courses.

Nina pitches in eagerly, "Yeah, Mom, we'll even help. And think how *great* it'll be for Gabby and Gampy, and Rittie and Bish, when they visit."

"But—" starts Dad.

I race on, "We'll get a big heater, it'll be like having her own thermostat, and don't forget there's a bathroom down there. It's better than sharing with us—you know how Nina clogs . . ." I stop as Nina looks warningly at me.

Mom says tentatively, "Raj? What do you think? If we really fix it up . . . ?" She's gazing into the distance; she's already planning it.

Nina reaches out and grips my hand.

Dad sighs heavily. "Maybe it is the best solution . . . if you think . . ."

Nina and I both go, "Yes!"

Mom wags her finger at us. "Hold it—I'll expect you

both to help, okay? With my new job, I'll have even less time than usual." She looks suddenly tired. "And I suppose I'll have to drop my writing course."

"It won't be too bad," says Dad, cheerfully. "We'll get in cleaners. Decorators, too, for that matter."

"Yeah," Nina and I say fervently.

"Raj, you can't get cleaners in without *tidying* first. Besides, we have to coordinate everything, and decorators do a terrible job of papering."

Nina and I exchange horrified glances. Mom and Dad papered the kitchen last year. They'd bought the wallpaper only five years before that. Dad was up on a chair holding on to the wallpaper, with water trickling down his arm, yelling, *It's not sticking.* Mom snapped, *Do I have to do everything myself?* and climbed up on the chair. Then she shrieked, *It's not prepasted! You bought wallpaper that's not prepasted!* And Dad said, *I didn't buy it, you did,* and Mom hollered, *Never mind who. Now what do we do?*

From the family room, we can hear Maya singing along with the closing bars of *Sesame Street.*

I nudge Nina and we creep upstairs to my room.

"Jeez!" I huff. "What on earth is Dad's freaking mother *like* . . . ?"

Nina just shakes her head, her eyes wide.

I frown. "I wonder what Dad feels about her . . . ?"

We start laughing. It's a joke in our house that whenever Mom asks Dad what he's feeling he always comes back with *I think.*

"Look, we've got to find out more about all this. I'll try

and talk to Mom, okay? And you keep your ears open—if Mom's on the phone to Rittie or Gabby . . ."

Nina grins. She has the most amazing knack for eaves-dropping.

She flings her arms around me. "At least we have our rooms. You were great, Tar. Thanks."

CHAPTER

6

I set my clock radio for early the next morning so I can talk to Mom, but I wake up even before it goes off. I spend a few minutes lazing in bed—will I see Jeff today? Maybe this time I'll say just the right thing, and . . . I jump as my radio comes on.

I dress quickly and rush downstairs to the kitchen. This is my best chance to get Mom alone—Dad's already gone to work, Maya won't be up for a while, and Nina never gets up until the last possible moment. There's no point even trying to talk to Dad, he's hopelessly vague, but if I can get Mom to stop being discreet and Marmee-ish . . .

"Hey, how come you're up already?" Mom hugs me and plants a series of kisses.

I go for the direct approach. "I want to talk to you. About Dad's mother. What's going on? Why's she coming now?"

Mom takes out some cereal bowls with one hand, opens the cutlery drawer with the other. "She must be lonely, dear—she's been widowed for years. And she hasn't seen your father in a while."

I digest that. Is that supposed to mean Dad's mother isn't interested in seeing Mom? Or us?

"Okay. So how come she's never been here before? And don't give me that bull you gave me years ago, about how busy she is."

Mom glances at me as she takes out the Cheerios and Weetabix. "Well, she is. She's a . . ." Mom pauses. ". . . a Very Capable Woman, with many demands on her time."

"Come on, Mom, I'm fifteen, and I'm not stupid. You keep saying I can talk to you about anything, and here you are, giving me the runaround."

Mom puts the cereal boxes down. "I'm sorry. I do want you to be able to talk to me about anything."

Bull's-eye. I manage to smother my satisfaction.

"It's just, she is Raj's mother, and whatever problems, er, differences, I may have . . . well, I don't want to influence you."

I raise an eyebrow. "What makes you think you can?"

"Brat." Mom taps my cheek.

"So what happened, Mom? Why didn't you get along?"

Mom's face is guarded. "Well, let's just say she wasn't . . . thrilled when Raj and I got married." She gets the milk jug out of the fridge.

"Yeah, yeah, I figured that. But why? Hey, you're nice and fair, aren't you?"

Mom turns around and snaps, "Don't be flip, Tara. Not all Indians are concerned about skin color—you should know that. Raj's parents are well educated, they're not the lower-class type." She bangs the milk down on the table.

Oh sure! It's fine for Mom to criticize the hypocrisies of Indian customs, but no one else can. And where does she get off with this class stuff anyway?

But I choke down my irritation and say in my most reasonable tone, "That's exactly my point—I don't know anything about them, and I want to. It's my family, and . . ."

Mom takes the orange-juice jug out of the fridge and clicks her tongue. "Wonderful. Three drops. Why can't you kids wash the jug?"

"It wasn't me, it's Nina. Here. I'll do it."

I wash the jug and get the orange-juice concentrate from the freezer.

"So talk, Mom. What's the family feud about?"

Mom's getting the peanut butter from the cupboard. She turns around, exasperated. "For goodness' sake, there's no *feud*, Tara. We just didn't get along."

"Yeah, but why?"

She's stiff again. "It's just . . . Raj's parents were very proud of being Indian and . . ."

"Oh, great!" Shades of Tolly!

Mom's mouth is tight. "Yes, well, they saw it as part and parcel of supporting the Independence movement." She spreads slices of bread on the cutting board and starts to slap on the peanut butter. "They felt they had to reject *everything* British—take the moral high ground."

"Give me a break!"

Mom grimaces slightly. "Well, it was their whole way of

life—their big *cause*." She flushes, hurries on, "Not that everyone in India wasn't for Independence; it's not as though my parents were *for* British rule. They've talked about how appallingly the British treated Indians—like dirt, worse than dirt—but . . ." She swallows. "Raj's parents, they were part of the committed inner circle—Mahatma Gandhi, the nonviolent demonstrations, everything. You know they even went to jail for it."

I can't quite repress my grin.

Mom wags her peanut-buttery knife at me. "Brat—it was civil disobedience, to overthrow oppression, and completely justified."

"Yeah, I know, I know. Martin Luther King used some of Gandhi's principles, and it's cool, but—"

Mom looks around. "Where's the strawberry jelly?"

I get it from the fridge.

"I still don't get what their problem was with you. You're not a Brit, you . . ." I stop. There's precious little Indian about Mom.

Mom shrugs disdainfully. "They wanted Raj to marry someone more Indian." She unscrews the lid and digs her peanut-buttery knife right into the jelly. It drives me crazy, but I bite my tongue. "And they wanted—no, *expected*—their son, us, to live in India."

"What?" I start to laugh. Yeah, that would go over big. Mom doesn't even believe in being a hyphenated Canadian. Home's home and it's here. That's why she gets so mad at Tolly and his kind.

"So what happened? Was there a fight?"

Mom claps the slices of bread together. "Let's just say they made it abundantly clear that a good little Indian woman ought to follow her husband to *his* home."

"Yeah, right! Like Dad didn't have a say in it. . . ." I trail off. Dad pretty much goes along with whatever Mom says.

Mom puts the sandwiches in the plastic containers and bangs the lids shut. She's almost talking to herself. "We discussed it before we got married; we *both* decided—it was *unthinkable* for me. Things are difficult in India. I'd left Bombay when I was thirteen; I'd lived in England and then here—did they want me to *never* belong? I had to survive, but"—Mom's voice has a trace of bitterness—"to Raj's parents, any westernized Indians had simply sold out to the oppressors."

"Oh, please!"

Mom's on a roll. "But it's not as though the Indian culture is just one thing. Bombay—Mumbai, they call it now—it's westernized, international, but it's India, too; and I can't help the way I was brought up—it was my parents' choice; but just because I don't *blindly* glorify the Indian culture, pretend it's all *perfect*, Raj's family . . ." She swallows. "It was his mother, mostly. As far as *she* was concerned, I lured their son away from India. It was awful for Raj. We were so happy, but . . ."

From upstairs, the toilet flushes.

Mom's head snaps up. "Goodness, that must be Maya. Tara, wash some apples, will you, dear?" She plugs in the kettle and dashes upstairs.

Mechanically, I wash the apples, then pour myself a bowl of cereal.

It's crazy. Indian enough, not Indian enough. Lines, boundaries, on every side. I'm not exotic enough for the *gee-I-love-your-culture* types like Tolly, but too Indian for the rednecks that yell *Paki*.

It comes rushing back, like a dark cloud. Samantha. In third grade. *I don't like Tara, she's black.*

Me staring at my arms. Not black. My own familiar skin, brown, smooth. Golden, Mom said. It didn't make sense.

Me, telling Mom. "I'm a person, not a color."

Mom was livid. She sailed into school and spoke to the teacher, then the principal. I hugged the superiority Mom wrapped around me and tried to console myself with the thought of Samantha getting into trouble.

But the principal ended up speaking to the whole class about same and different, how it didn't matter about the color of your skin, and I just wanted to shrivel up and disappear. *Don't look at me, look at Samantha, she's the one.* Samantha apologized, but she said it again the next time she got mad. Except that time I didn't tell Mom.

Mom comes back to the kitchen and starts wiping the counter. The kettle is noisier now, gurgling as it heats. Nina's banging around upstairs. She'll be down soon, and Maya, too, even though she insists on dressing herself.

I ask my question abruptly. "Mom, I assume Dad's mother speaks English, right? But . . . but how well?"

A strange look ripples across Mom's face. "As a matter of fact, she speaks perfect English."

Something hangs in the air unsaid.

I hesitate, then push on. "But you still haven't told me—what's she *like*?"

41

Mom throws a couple of Earl Grey teabags into her pot. Her face is guarded. "Well, in a way she's, she's a bit like Maya."

"Maya?" My shoulders come down. "But Maya's so . . . cute."

The rumbling of the kettle softens, the quiet before the fury.

"Yes, but she's also . . ."—Mom pauses—". . . formidable."

I try to digest the word—it's bricklike, solid.

The kettle shrieks and Mom pours water into the teapot.

As Maya comes downstairs, singing, Mom lowers her voice and says hastily, "Tara, I hope what I've said about your grandmother isn't going to influence . . ." She catches my eye. "Okay, okay. Look, let's just try to be *nice* to her."

Then Nina thunders downstairs, complaining that she can't find clean socks, and I escape to my room.

It's strange, all this long-ago drama—it makes me feel like I'm looking through the wrong end of binoculars.

But it's still patchy, the family saga, a jigsaw puzzle with pieces missing. There's the small woman in the photograph. There's being too Indian, or not being Indian enough. There's the hero of the Independence movement. There's *formidable*.

And shining over it all, like a welcoming rainbow, is *be nice to her*.

CHAPTER
7

But it isn't until the evening that I discover the horror lurking behind Mom's pious wish to be *nice*.

After dinner, Mom gathers the battalion together and barks out her orders for the weekend. Turns out, she's *deadly* serious about cleaning out that basement room and fixing it up like the flipping Hilton—and she's even deadlier serious about holding Nina and me to the devil's bargain we made to keep our rooms.

So it starts. Hell.

Saturday is a blur of boxes, bags, dust, and mess. We sneeze and scowl as we cart the junk from the spare room to the rest of the house—six boxes end up in my room. Mom can't throw out *anything*; she even insists on keeping my art folder from grade one, for God's sake.

By the end of the day the room is finally cleared, but the walls are a grimy, puky pink and the carpet is ragged—it'll take a miracle to get it decent, never mind gorgeous.

As we collapse in the family room after pizza, Mom wearily but unrelentingly plans the next stage of the campaign—wallpaper, carpet, furniture; even giving the entire freaking house a thorough cleaning. Dad looks seriously depressed. Nina and I gape at each other in dumb misery. Why, *why* is that awful woman coming? Why can't she just keep up the feud?

Sunday, I'm so desperate to get out of cleaning that I spend hours over my math homework and practice my violin until my arms drop. But the minute Mom hears me stop playing . . .

I'm so exhausted that I sleep through my alarm the next morning, and it's a mad dash to get ready for school. I can't even sound off to Erin, because she has band practice Mondays. I tear into the lobby just as the bell goes and almost run into Tolly putting up a giant banner. *Greetings from Around the World.*

I snort. Too late for my *drop dead* in Hindi.

Tolly turns, his bushy eyebrows raised. I avoid his eye and race to my English class. It would have to be on the other side of the building, on the second floor.

The class has already started as I slide in, breathless. Good thing it's only Ms. Gelder. She's one of the younger teachers, and she never freaks out if you're a bit late.

I sigh as I grab the empty desk near the back—school's actually going to be restful after the weekend.

Doug's complaining about his mark on the last assignment. We had to write a story, and I got an A—but I love creative writing, and Doug stinks at it.

Then I notice. Jeff's next to me. He grins and I sort of puff and grin back, swipe my hand through my hair.

Ms. Gelder's saying, "Well, Doug, you should enjoy the next assignment. It's important for you to explore fiction as a medium for your voice and to stretch your imagination, but it is also a skill to write something factual in an accessible and interesting manner."

Doug goes, "Yes," but most of us groan. I glance at Jeff. He's looking at me. I flush and turn away.

Ms. Gelder continues. "So—what I want you to do now is interview someone in this class so you can later write a biography on him or her. Please include their likes, dislikes, and . . ."

I catch Nadia's eye and she grins and nods.

"Not someone you know well," Ms. Gelder goes on. "Just work with the person sitting next to you."

My heart somersaults. Yes! There is a God! Jeff smiles shyly at me, and I moisten my lips, smile back. Thank goodness I grabbed a shower this morning.

Then everyone's shuffling desks together.

"So—you want to go first, or . . . ?" Jeff awkwardly pushes up the sleeves of his brown sweater.

"You go." I furtively eye his hands, the fine down on his arms.

"No, you go."

I laugh. "So why'd you ask?"

He shrugs, half grinning.

Suddenly, it clicks. Maybe he's shy, too—he just moved here from another province. That's a load in itself, let alone getting to know a strange girl.

"Okay, me first," I say. "Name. Duhh! Jeffrey MacKinley. So, Jeff, you're from Vancouver, right?"

"Yeah. Sort of. I lived there for four years, but I was born in Halifax. I've moved around a lot because my father's in the military. Army brat."

I say brightly, "Hey, it must be neat to travel around." I realize how stupid that is even before I see his mouth tighten.

"How would you like to move just when you've settled in and made friends?"

Ouch. "I guess that was dumb of me."

Jeff half puts his hand out towards me, then pulls it back. "Hey, no, I didn't mean that. A lot of people think the same, really. Like my grandfather." He grins. "He was army, too. Joined up for the travel, as a matter of fact. He was born in Scotland, and he went everywhere with the British army—Egypt, Burma. Even spent a few years in India. He loved it there."

"Hey, cool."

"Yeah, he immigrated here after World War II." He pauses. "He's in Halifax now. I miss him."

"Sounds like you're close to him."

"Yeah. He's pretty great. We have these long discussions about life—everything. I mean, I can talk to him. My father, now . . ." He shakes his head, then is silent.

"So, how d'you like living here?" I ask tentatively. "Sick of people asking?"

He smiles and shrugs. "Nah, it's okay. It still feels kinda strange."

"You should get someone to show you around, Jeff; Ottawa's a neat town."

He looks up eagerly.

Blood rushes to my face. "Yeah, sure, I could, if . . . if you want. . . ." I can't believe I actually said that.

Jeff's smile leaps at me. "I'd like that, Tara. A lot. There's no one my age where I live, except this guy Steve. The only thing we have in common is hockey."

I groan slightly.

"What? What's wrong with that?"

I grin. "Jeff, tell me you're not a dumb jock. Please."

"Hey, do I look like a dumb jock?"

"Well, jock, no . . . but dumb, well . . ."

Jeff laughs.

Then we're on a roll, talking easily. I find out his parents divorced two years ago and his mother moved to Ontario, but he stayed with his father because of school. He has an older sister who's going to university out west, and he's thinking about being a vet. He loves animals, but they can't have any because his father has allergies. It's pretty obvious that he and his father don't get along—Jeff says half-sneeringly, *He's always the Colonel, even at home.* It's sure different from how he talked about his grandfather.

"Okay, your turn, Tara. Tell me everything." He quirks an eyebrow. "Especially about the skeletons lurking in your closet."

I grin. That's how Erin described this grandmother business, and it sort of fits. I tell Jeff about Dad's mother coming from India but avoid the more controversial elements.

"So—does your grandmother speak Indian?"

I look at him. "It's not Indian, it's Hindi. And, yeah, she does."

"Do you?"

My stomach sinks. Great. Another Tolly-type conversation. "No. Never have." It comes out belligerent.

Jeff frowns slightly. "What'd I say wrong?"

"Nothing." I scrape a stain on my jeans with my fingernail, then blurt out, "It's just . . . I get sick of people assuming that because my parents came from India I should be all Indian, and different, and . . ."

"Hey, all I said was . . ." His blue eyes are puzzled.

"Yeah, well, it's just, sometimes people try to . . . try to shove me into their idea of who they think I am, and . . ."

"I didn't mean—"

"Forget it."

Why, *why* did I spaz? It's the Tolly thing—it's still fresh, and I'm hypersensitive.

Jeff says slowly, "I guess you get fed up with people treating you like you're the expert on everything Indian, huh?"

I look up. "Yeah. It makes me feel . . . labeled, somehow, even though, mostly, it's so . . ."

"Well intentioned!"

"Yeah. Shining, polite interest."

Jeff grins. "White liberal guilt!"

I laugh.

Jeff continues, "My best friend in Vancouver, his family was from China. He got it all the time. It stank. He'd never even been to China. I suppose you've never been to India, either."

Now that I know he isn't trying to slot me into a category, we're easy again. I tell him about Maya, Dad, Nina's BFT, and even about Mom's feminist rants and dumb accents.

A gleam comes into Jeff's eyes. "Hey, I could try my Scottish accent on her. My grandfather still has a thick one."

I squeal, "No. You wouldn't dare."

"You bet I would."

"Too late. She's been watching Dr. Finlay on TV and keeps coming out with *Och! The bonnie wee laddie!* It's not funny, Jeff."

We start as the bell rings. Neither of us has made any notes.

"So—we're going to have to get together to finish this." Jeff sounds shy again. He scratches his head and turns red. "Some evening this week, maybe?"

I want to shout, *Yes! Yes!* I manage a cool, "Sounds good."

"Your place?" he asks eagerly.

I hesitate, tuck my hair behind my ear. I mean, my family is weird at the best of times, and now, with this visit . . .

I try frantically to think up a good excuse as we exchange phone numbers, but Jeff seems really keen. Anyway, it's probably better than going to his place. . . .

CHAPTER

8

Big mistake! Because now there's only a bit over two weeks to go, and not one corner of our house remains unmolested by Mom's cleaning fetish.

Jeff's due after supper on Wednesday, and I hope and hope that when he arrives the family will be in the basement—or anywhere, just so they're out of sight.

But, no, it's like they've *conspired* to humiliate me. Mom's in the kitchen, up on a chair excavating one of the cupboards, looking like a scruffy flamingo in her grubby pink leggings. Maya is wiggling in and out of one of the lower cupboards, and Nina, her hair wild and tangled, is scowling over her French verbs. I should have insisted on going to his house—I bet his father is at least *normal*.

When the doorbell rings, I run to the door. If I can sneak Jeff into the family room, maybe he won't have to . . .

Jeff smiles and looks a bit uncomfortable.

"Hi," I say. "Come on in."

A loud crash from the kitchen. Then Mom shouts, "Blast! Tara, quick, I need a hand."

My heart sinks down past my toes, through the floor, deep into the subsoil.

I say apologetically, "The cleaning—for the grandmother's visit!"

Jeff follows me into the kitchen.

Cake pans are scattered on the floor, and Mom's struggling with another pile. "Tara, take—"

"Mom, I've got work. . . ."

"Here, let me." Jeff takes the pile.

Mom beams down at him. "*Thank* you, m'dear." The posh British accent. "You're too kind."

Jeff half grins, then glances at me, his eyes bright. "Och, it's nuthin'. Yerr wellcome."

My jaw drops.

Mom squeals delightedly, "Och, he's a bonnie wee Scottish laddie!"

"Aye, Ms. Mehta." Jeff's face is a curious mixture of shy and eager. "My grandfather's from the Highlands."

"Och, the Highlands! Which bonnie parrrt?" cries Mom.

She continues to pass him stuff from the cupboard as she grills him about his life in the *worst* Scottish accent.

I just want to die.

Then Nina clears her throat and introduces herself, her eyes raking him for details to giggle over with her friends, and Maya insists that he admire how *thor-ough-ly* she's sorting out her cupboard. When I think it *can't* get any worse, Dad erupts from the basement, all sweaty in his holey Blue Jays T-shirt, his hands covered in grout.

I stand against the wall, my arms tightly crossed. It's like my family is a giant freaking amoeba engulfing any foreign body dumb enough to stray in.

As soon as Mom's cupboard is empty, I drag Jeff into the family room before she can start another.

I mumble, "Look, I'm sorry about that. . . ."

Jeff's shoulders shake with laughter.

"It's not funny, Jeff." I roll my eyes. "And why did you have to encourage her, anyway?"

"But it's research, Tara." He's still laughing.

"Cut it out!" I whack his arm. "She's bad enough without you—"

"Hey, come on! I think your family's great. I can't imagine my father unbending enough to . . . You're lucky—"

"Yeah, right."

"Oh, lighten up, Tara. . . ." Jeff's arm brushes across my back for a few seconds.

My face flames. But my heart rises marginally from the subsoil.

After we finish our work, we actually manage to get some time to just talk. We're so easy together, it's pretty great—even though Mom interrupts with more Scottish banter and a plateful of god-awful homemade cookies she's thawed for us, and Normy wanders in and rubs against Jeff, until he picks her up and feeds her tiny bits of the cookies.

It's late when Jeff finally leaves. At the door he reminds me, "Don't forget, you promised to show me around. Next weekend, maybe?"

The look in his eyes makes me flush, but then Mom shrills from the kitchen, "Ye be surrre to come back agin, laddie," and Jeff calls back, "Aye, I will, Ms. Mehta, ferrr surre," which pretty much kills the mood.

And now the countdown to the visit really begins in earnest.

All week, I babysit Maya uncomplainingly. I scrub and clean. I even bite my tongue as Mom oscillates from Marmee to banshee, rushing between her job and the cleaning, decorating, and shopping. Hey, on Saturday, I'll get time off for good behavior to hang out with Jeff, right?

Yeah, right! We have a huge fight, but Mom flatly refuses to give me even a crappy half-day off. I call Jeff and cancel; I rave and rant about the cleaning, promise to show him around the first weekend I'm free—but what if he thinks I'm trying to get out of it?

The weekend passes in a whirl of misery and grime. I scrub walls like Cinder-flipping-ella, while my hands shrivel into prunes. Even Dad's good humor flags, and he slips momentarily from his soothing, supporting role. I hear snatches of them arguing: Mom's voice squeaking with indignation, *Three weeks' notice, if that isn't just . . .* and Dad's, unexpectedly loud, *I asked you, why didn't you . . .*

By now, I'm painstakingly particular about my homework; I stretch it out for hours. When Mom mutters, I snap, *D'you want me to flunk?* Nina, too, catches on, and her marks skyrocket. I also practice my violin like crazy. Poor Hélène is super-impressed—she thinks I've developed a real passion. I'm amazed at how good I'm starting to sound.

Then it's less than two weeks to go, and to our relief, Dad insists on hiring wallpaper hangers. But all he gets at short notice are two burly, beery guys, Ronnie, and—don't ask why—Twinkie, who flash their cracks every time they bend over. Mom shudders but is too tired to protest.

School is now a wonderful rest. It's also the only time I get to see Jeff. We hang out after class a couple of times, but it's not the same as actually doing something together. I don't know if he quite believes me when I tell him Mom hasn't done an accent in ages. Erin is totally disgusted because Mom's too busy to cook Indian food. *I'm in withdrawal*, she moans.

Then we roll into the final week before D-day, and the new carpet is laid, but Mom still shops like fury for the perfect towels and duvet, while I resentfully polish the banister and babysit Maya. Nina's majorly miffed, because for once Mom won't let her have her horde over, in case they wreck a room that's already DONE—Mom actually says this as though it has been blessed and sanctified.

Nina and I can't decide who we hate more—the grandmother, Mom, or even Dad, for giving in to Mom's neurotic demands. We share every scrap of information about the dreaded grandmother, which isn't a lot. All we get out of Dad is that she's in her early seventies and her name's Savitri, after an Indian goddess. And nothing from Mom— I avoid her like the plague, but even Nina can't overhear any juicy tidbits, because Mom discreetly vanishes to her room every time she phones Rittie.

The only person more or less unaffected by all this is Maya. She glides through the chaos in her own sweet little world, but somehow she manages to get Mom to respond to her needs—she just expects it. I begin to understand Mom calling her *formidable*.

CHAPTER
9

By Tuesday, three days before the arrival of *Your Grand-mother*, we're all totally frazzled.

I drag my heels coming home from school, but when I open the front door, I'm surprised by the unexpected silence. No clattering or banging, no shrill voices. Mom must be off somewhere with Nina and Maya, thank goodness.

But as I head into the kitchen, there's Mom—sitting at the table, like it's the temple of doom.

"Hi, pet," she says listlessly.

"Hi," I say curtly. "Where are Nina and Maya?"

"At the park." She smiles weakly. "Boy, I'm pooped."

Tough. Am I supposed to feel sorry for her?

"And what's that about?" Mom inquires acidly. "The eye rolling, the look of disdain."

I can't stop myself. "Well, who asked you to do all this cleaning?"

Mom's eyes glitter. "Thank you, Tara. Aren't you just

56

charming? Thank you so much for all your support and sympathy."

It's like a dam bursts. "You're the one who wants to impress Dad's mom—we don't give a damn. And if you weren't so horribly disorganized, the house would never get like this in the first place—you make everyone crazy with your mess, and now you're driving us demented with your cleaning."

Mom sits upright, eyes blazing. Oh jeez. I wait for the thunderbolt.

Unexpectedly, the fire fades and she slumps back in her chair. She looks . . . just like Gabby when Mom lights into her about standing up to Gampy. I shift uncomfortably.

Mom says stiffly, "I'm sorry if this housecleaning is disturbing, but I want the house to be presentable for Your Grandmother. I'm perfectly aware that I'm not the world's best housekeeper, and I'm sorry if it bothers you." Her mouth is oddly vulnerable.

I sit down. "Sorry, Mom." Tentatively, I stroke the back of her hand.

She turns it up and grips mine, flashing a grin that's a shadow of her usual cheerful one.

It suddenly hits me. Dad's mother will actually *be* here in three days, and she's Mom's *mother-in-law*—my mother has a history I know practically nothing about.

It's starting to get dark out, but we still haven't turned on the lights.

I ask softly, "Mom, what . . . what actually happened when you got married? Why are you . . . I mean, how did she treat you?"

Mom sighs. "Oh, it wasn't any one thing that was so terrible. It was more . . . silences, this air of disapproval. It was pretty constant." Mom's talking wearily, almost to herself. "It was . . . it was as though I was *unworthy* of belonging to this great family that had done so much for the freedom struggle. I felt so . . . unwelcome. An outsider. She'd talk in Hindi to Raj at every opportunity, even though she knew I didn't understand it well."

I stiffen.

"She was always contemptuous of me." Despite the gloomy light I see Mom's jaw clench. "Because I didn't wear saris or *salwar khameez* all the time, or *bindi*. You know . . ." Mom touches her forehead to indicate the dot worn there. "And because I didn't like to eat with my hands—she deliberately wouldn't put out any cutlery. She was so cold, because I didn't know the ins and outs. Or care about them."

"Like what?"

"Oh, most of it was so silly. To me, anyway. Things I never thought mattered. If I called her Mummy and forgot the *ji* to show respect. The way she corrected me—she never shouted; it would've been a relief if she had. It was her coldness, it was icy. Raj was so . . . so caught in the middle, trying to keep things smooth. But of course he's a man, he didn't notice a lot of it." She's back there, caught in the past.

I don't move.

"Until her comments about Mom and Dad. She came right out with it. Raj was furious."

My neck prickles. "Gabby and Gampy? What about them?"

Mom draws in a long breath. "Well, after that . . . that episode about us not living there, she finally gave vent to her true feelings. Scorn. What else could she expect from the daughter of people who'd sat pretty through the freedom struggle?"

"What?" My voice is squeaky. "What did she mean by that?"

Mom says tightly, "Oh, they weren't active enough for her majesty, not *revolutionaries* like she'd been. Also, they lived a western lifestyle. And Dad had worked for the Indian Civil Service, under the British." She glances quickly at me, says defensively, "Many Indians did. They were needed to keep the government going after the British left, but just because they weren't directly involved with the protests—"

"That's so freaking stupid!" There's a sharp taste in my mouth. I mean, Gabby and Gampy bug me at times, but I love them. "Shoving her values down everyone's throat. It's like . . . it's like Tolly."

"Tolly? Your teacher?" Mom gets up and switches on the lights. "What about him?"

Uh-oh. I'm about to make up some excuse, but Mom's eyes are returning to the present. And I want to pummel her back to the way she normally is—it's maddening, but at least it's familiar.

So I tell her.

It's actually a relief to see Mom in one of her dignified snits. She sits straight, eyes flashing with righteous indignation.

"Clearly, your teacher is laboring under the misapprehension that if you're not white you must necessarily, therefore, be of a *different* culture. Partly, it's an attempt to *exotify* differences, but it's offensive nevertheless, because it thrusts an identity upon you that may or may not be accurate. . . ."

When she's finally done, she leans forward eagerly and says, "Tara, I'd be *happy* to have a *gentle little word* with him . . ."

"No, Mom, *no*. I can handle it."

I manage to get rid of her by offering to take care of dinner while she lies down. But it's easier than usual to talk her out of fixing Tolly—which kind of freaks me out.

When Nina and Maya get home, I settle Maya in the family room with her coloring book and pull Nina into the kitchen. I tell her everything as I thaw the spaghetti sauce.

Nina's eyes go round. "Jeez. Dad's mother sounds like a total *bitch*."

I nod grimly. "Grade A, five star. I mean, if Mom's this frantic *now*, what's she going to be like when his mother actually *gets* here?"

Nina gapes at me.

"Look, it's up to you and me. This is *our* territory. There's *no way* we're letting her rule the roost."

"Yeah," says Nina. "We'll show her who's boss." She rubs her hands gleefully.

But it's almost a game to her; I don't think she gets it. And Mom and Dad are so in denial.

It looks like I'm the only one who truly understands what's going to happen when that woman finally gets here.

All hell is going to break loose.

CHAPTER
10

It's D-day, at last. The house is squeaky clean and super-tidy—almost like a funeral parlor, with the flowers Mom's stuck everywhere. We're sitting around the kitchen table eating pizza. No one had the energy to cook.

Dad insists that we all go to the airport after dinner to meet his mother. I can think of a dozen other places I'd rather be, like, say, at the dentist's getting fillings, but I know it's safer not to argue.

We eat silently, frozen in the glossy magazine picture of the ideal home. Except no one's smiling.

Then Nina breaks the silence. "Hey, Dad, what're we supposed to call her? Your mother?"

For once I'm glad of Nina's blurts.

Dad shifts in his chair, his face stiff. Is he at all aware of what we feel about his mother—how much we hate her?

"I guess . . . er, well, I think, Naniji."

"Yes." Mom smiles determinedly. "'Naniji' sounds just right."

"Nah-ni-ji! Nah-ni-ji!" Maya drums her spoon on her plate.

"And, girls . . ." Dad's face is strained. "Please try extra hard to be polite. Remember that in India you're supposed to respect your elders. Her ideas of what's, I mean, your grandmother, er, Naniji, will expect . . ."

Fury jolts through me.

Quick as a whip, I lean forward, but Mom interjects, "I'm sure the girls will be *perfectly* polite. *Won't* you, girls? You treat *everyone* with respect, *don't* you?" She's italicizing desperately.

"Nah-ni-ji! Nah-ni-ji!" chants Maya.

I snap on my fakest smile. "Don't worry, Dad. We'll be *excruciatingly* polite."

"Yeah, *agonizingly*," says Nina, with a glint in her eye.

"Now, girls," starts Dad.

He looks so hounded, I have to say, "Oh, Dad, don't look so . . . so constipated."

The laughter shatters the artificial gloss.

Dad sighs. "Okay, okay, just be your normal selves."

"Raj, my love," says Mom, eyes twinkling. "Don't you think that's going rather too far?"

"Hey, whaddya mean?" Nina switches to Mom's posh British accent, "I hev splen-did manners. *Syu-perb*."

Mom wags her finger at us. "Just remember, no BFT."

Nina grins at me and lets out a big burp.

"Nina!" says Mom.

"But that's not bodily-function *talk*."

"Okay, let me spell it out. No BFT and no BFN. That's bodily-function noises. Got it?"

"But what about a fart?" I ask, my face shiningly innocent. "Everyone has to fart sometimes; it's natural. You mean we can't *fart* in front of Naniji?"

"Yeah, what d'you expect us to do, Mom?" asks Nina. "Explode?"

Mom's face sinks into her hands.

I say, "It's okay, Mom; we'll make sure we say *excuse me* properly. . . ."

"Pahdon me for pahssing gas," says Nina in her poshest voice. "Hey, what's Hindi for *fart*, Dad?"

"You don't really expect me to tell you, do you?"

"Okay," I say. "How's *Nahniji, pahdon me for brrreaking wind.*"

We're all laughing too hard—with almost a touch of hysteria.

Then Dad looks at the clock and says we'd better clear up. And the blanket of gloom descends again.

After Mom runs upstairs three times, once to change her clothes, twice to change her shoes, we finally get into the van and head to the airport.

Of course we're way too early. *Well, there might have been a traffic jam*, Dad mumbles as we hang around the Customs doors.

Everyone's on edge except Maya. She's having a great time climbing up and down a chair. Mom keeps twitching Maya's dress straight, smoothing Nina's shirt or my collar, and talking too fast—about the weather, how unreliable the airlines are, how Customs can be so slow, and how tiring the journey from India is. Such a long way to come.

Dad paces up and down, faster and faster. Nina slumps into a chair, moans, *This is so borrring*, and then sulks when Dad snaps at her.

I lean against a pillar, my arms tightly crossed. *Why* are we all being dragged into this charade for someone who never wanted to see us before? What kind of person practically cuts off her son just because he marries someone she disapproves of?

Well, I've had enough. She's not my mother-in-law, and I don't care squat for her antiquated ideas. We can make her life pretty miserable, Nina and I—we'll have her catching the first plane back. You'd better watch it, lady; the line's drawn.

Mom and Dad are now craning to look as people start coming through the Customs doors. Every time the doors open, my heart thumps.

Then Dad cries, "There she is!"

Mom smooths her hair, pulls Maya off the chair, and straightens her dress.

"Mom, you're holding too tight," wails Maya.

"Sorry, sweetie," says Mom breathlessly.

My heart pounds steadily. All right, Grandmother from Hell, I'm waiting.

I now make out to whom Mom and Dad are waving. I take a long, hard look.

Small, slightly plump. She's wearing a wheat-colored *salwar khameez*, the Indian tunic and baggy pants. It's stylishly cut, looks tailor-made. Dark hair with a fair bit of gray, pulled back low into a tidy, elegant bun. Two small bags and a camel-colored coat in the cart. When Gabby and Gampy come they bring tons of luggage—bursting with presents for us. She pushes her cart with decision, no crippled crab-walk—she looks healthy and strong, younger than seventy. Her face is severe, but I don't see the fierce revolutionary Mom talked about.

Then she notices Dad and Mom, and she breaks into a smile. It's like Maya's—slow to start, but transforming. She moves quickly towards Dad and hugs him hard.

He folds her in his arms, says in a funny voice, "Mum-myji."

I won't hug her, I won't.

She pulls away from Dad and looks up at him. No. Her lips can't be trembling. She turns to Mom. Yes, her mouth is all puckered.

"Rohini," she says. A tear rolls down her cheek as she hugs Mom.

Mom is crying, too. It's a long hug.

What? What the hell is going on?

Dad's mother pulls away. She wipes her face and steadies her lips. She is short. I knew that from the picture, but I'm still surprised at how Mom towers above her. She holds on to Mom's hand, grips it desperately. It's almost as though her eyes are saying *please*.

Then Naniji hugs Maya. She hugs Nina.

She turns to me. I'm ready for battle but there is none.

I can't help it. I let her hug me, and slackly put my arms around her. She's so much smaller than I am.

She is shaking.

CHAPTER
11

It's totally bizarre—all these weeks of living in hell and now, suddenly, it's sweetness and light.

The drive home from the airport is like something out of *Little Women*. Mom actually offers Naniji the front seat but she says, *No, no, Rohini, your place is with Raj.* I think I see Mom's face twitch.

I get into the back seat fast. I'm not sitting with Naniji. She sits in front of me, small and serene, with Nina and Maya beside her. Mom talks animatedly all the way home, eagerly pointing out sights that can't be seen because it's too dark. Naniji responds, all appreciative. No thick Indian accent, just a trace. She speaks English perfectly, an old-fashioned kind. I can't catch Nina's eye.

Dad keeps asking questions about the trip and about his brother in India. Naniji answers and talks about old neighbors, stopping scrupulously to explain to Mom who's who.

Then we reach the house. It's lit up like Christmas.

66

And it's *showtime.*

As Mom and Dad give the tour, I watch Naniji, trying to catch traces of the person who heaped scorn all over Mom and Gabby and Gampy. No tears now. She's small, but there's something about her face, some sort of presence— did she really cry at the airport?

She's a determinedly appreciative audience—everything is *wonderful* or *beautiful.* She doesn't exude like Mom, but she says it with finality, like a stamp of official, irrefutable approval.

She's impressed with the house. *My, what a beautiful big house. It's wonderful to see you doing so well, Raj.* A pause. *And Rohini, of course.*

Her room is *wonderful and beautiful.* It really does look great. From the wallpaper—white with small blue and yellow flowers, hung more or less straight by the crack-flashing Ronnie and Twinkie—to the bright-yellow duvet cover, the flowers on the pine dresser, the blue lamp, and the white wicker rocker, plump with yellow silk cushions, everything is shining, earnest, and polite.

The only thing you *don't* see is the mayhem we went through.

Mercifully, Naniji refuses all offers of food and goes straight to bed. I hear the hiss of relief that escapes Mom. She looks exhausted—only her smile lingers in a Cheshire-cattish way. I rub her back gently as we go upstairs.

Saturday morning, I head slowly for the kitchen. Yesterday was way weird, but at least there wasn't a lot of it. Now there's a whole day ahead. The whole *visit*—no return date—looming.

Naniji is sitting at the kitchen table. Mom's got it laid with everything straight, instead of the usual slap-me-down. And Mom's actually making fresh-squeezed orange juice. She bought the juicer years ago and used it only once, because it was too much work. *Why* is she doing this? She still looks tired.

I give her a quick hug and say deliberately, "Fresh-squeezed, wow! What's the occasion?"

Mom flushes slightly.

"Good morning, Tara," says Naniji. She's wearing another *salwar khameez*, gray with burgundy, quiet, discreet. Her eyes are clear and rested; her smile is well modulated, just like her voice. There isn't a trace of yesterday's weakness at the airport—she looks strong and self-assured, and a bit stern. I bet she doesn't cry often.

"Mummyji, can I get you some more juice?" asks Mom.

"No, thank you, Rohini, that was just right." She turns to me. "I feel terribly spoiled. I slept so soundly. Everything is most comfortable. That duvet, is that what you call it? I've never slept under one before—so warm and soft. And your mummyji won't let me do anything. I'm not used to being waited on like this."

Mom says, "It's nothing, Mummyji. It's my pleasure."

They both smile—gracious smiles with the lips closed.

Oh, give me a break!

Dad comes into the kitchen and kisses Mom and Naniji.

As I reach for the cornflakes, Mom says, "Tara, love, I'm making pancakes. I want your naniji to try some real Canadian maple syrup."

"It sounds wonderful," says Naniji. *Beam, beam.*

68

Yeah, well, she doesn't fool me with all that smiley stuff. She may not have freaked out yet because we don't have pictures of blue Indian gods with multiple arms, but there's something about her eyes—they're controlling. Hard.

Maya comes into the kitchen dragging her blanket.

Naniji's smile is genuine this time. "Maya, come and sit with your nani." She holds out one arm.

Ha! Reality check. Maya never takes to people quickly.

Maya looks at Naniji gravely, measuring her. Then she breaks into her sunrise smile and climbs up on Naniji's lap. Naniji gives her a tidy, contained kiss, and Maya sits there like a queen, looking perfectly at home. Jeez! If I didn't love that kid so much, I'd shake her.

Normy wanders in, stares unblinkingly at Naniji, then turns her back and waddles away contemptuously, gut swaying from side to side. Way to go, Normy!

It's uncanny, looking at Maya in Naniji's lap. They're so alike—the same wide forehead, firm mouth, small straight nose, the same solid cheeks and strong chin. Every feature is deliberately and carefully in the right place, and they both have the same direct, see-everything gaze.

Mom puts the jug of juice on the table and starts the pancakes.

"Need help, Ro?" asks Dad.

"No thanks, love. I can manage. You sit and talk to Mummyji."

The traditional womanly thing! Oh, vomit! That's a first for Mom.

Nina bounces in and sits down.

"Fresh-squeezed juice? Mmm. How wonderful, Mother."

Nina? What the *heck?* I stare at her, but she doesn't even notice.

Naniji starts asking Nina and me questions about school and stuff. I answer as briefly as possible, my tone scrupulously polite but unmistakably dismissive. Dad frowns, but I ignore him. *I haven't forgotten the last few weeks. I haven't forgotten what Mom told me about her.*

Naniji raises her eyebrows slightly, but turns to Nina.

I watch Mom. She's actually following a recipe in *The Joy of Cooking.* I wait for her to fling in something bizarre, but she measures everything carefully, and the pancakes are perfect.

"Delicious, Rohini," says Naniji. "You know, I've only read about pancakes and maple syrup, but I've never had them before. Your mummyji is a wonderful cook—isn't she, girls?"

Beam, beam, all round, even Maya. What is this—an episode of *Leave It to Beaver?* I squint at Nina, *What the heck are you doing?* She mouths *What?* and turns away, scowling.

Naniji looks at me penetratingly. I raise my eyebrows and stare back. *This is my house, lady, you're not going to intimidate* me.

She swallows, and manufactures a fake smile. "I hear you play an instrument, Tara. It's the violin, isn't it? Your daddyji says you've been practicing a lot lately."

"Mmm," I grunt.

"It's an invaluable skill, learning to play an instrument. When I was your age I played the sitar. It still gives me great pleasure." She turns to Dad. "Do the girls know sitar music?"

Dad shifts uncomfortably. "No, no, they don't."

Naniji's face is carefully neutral, but she's blinking too hard. She'd better not try that superior Indian stuff here.

"I'm afraid there aren't any competent sitar teachers in Ottawa, to our knowledge," says Mom, with a hint of her British accent.

Yeah, right! Mom wouldn't know a competent sitar player if she fell over one.

Mom continues, "It's a most difficult instrument, girls. Your naniji is quite accomplished. It's a shame you couldn't bring it here, Mummyji."

I almost choke on my pancake. Dad's the only one in the family who actually likes sitar music—Mom says it sounds like dying cats.

Naniji smiles politely. "Never mind. But I would like to hear you play, Tara. Will you play something for me after breakfast?" Her tone is polite but commanding.

"I'm afraid I don't perform for strangers," I say, smoothly.

Naniji twitches. Her eyes flash.

Dad's face ripples with shock. "Tara," he snaps. "That is out of line."

Mom's laugh is measured and controlled. "You know how children are about playing in front of others, Mummyji."

Children! I glare at her.

Naniji says, "It's all right. I'd forgotten how I used to feel when people asked me to play when I was that age." But she doesn't look at me again.

Nina pipes up. "I'll play you something. I still know some piano pieces pretty well."

She's such a freaking Judas! Anyway, the only piece she still plays is "Thunder and Lightning," because it's hideously noisy.

"That will be lovely, Nina."

I push my chair away from the table, scraping it harshly.

"I'm going out for a bit. See you later."

"Tara, dear, your naniji just got here." There's a warning edge to Mom's gracious voice. "Don't you think you should spend some time at home?"

For a fraction of a second I teeter on the brink of *bite me*, but I don't particularly want to be grounded for life.

Naniji says, "No, Rohini, please. I don't want *anyone* to change their lives because of me. But before you go, Tara, I want to give you some little things I picked up for you."

She glides to the hallway and down the stairs.

I roll my eyes. Mom darts me a furious look.

Dad says thinly, "Tara, watch it."

In a way it's awful seeing that look in his eyes—hurt and angry. Well, tough. I cross my arms tight. I'm not joining this pathetic little charade.

When Naniji comes back up the stairs, she puts small packages on the table. Very small. Nina's eyes gloom over. Ha! The bubble's burst for her. I bet whatever it is stinks.

"This is for you, Rohini," Naniji hands Mom two packages. "And for you Raj, Nina, my little Maya, and Tara."

We all get two, even Dad, but she barely looks at me as she gives me mine. They're hard and knobbly, wrapped up in magenta tissue paper. I unfold the smaller package. Dangling pearl earrings.

Mom gasps, "Oh, Mummyji, they're beautiful." She's gaping at diamond earrings and six gold bangles.

"Oh, how *gorgeous*," squeaks Nina. She has red earrings and two silver bangles.

I open my other package. Two silver bangles. Maya has small gold earrings and silver bangles. Dad has a pair of gold cuff links.

"Thanks, Naniji," squeals Nina. "I just love them. What kind of stone is it?"

Turns out it's rubies.

"Papaji's watch," says Dad, in a funny voice.

Maya gives Naniji a big hug and a noisy smack on the cheek.

"Mummyji, we can't let you do this," says Mom. "It's *far* too extravagant."

Naniji smiles. With the eyes as well as the lips, this time. "It's my pleasure. I'm so glad you like it."

I have to admit, my pearl earrings are really gorgeous. Small, but beautiful. Exuding good taste and discretion— like Naniji. Like our gaggy little family.

Mom hesitates a fraction of a second, then hugs Naniji. Naniji pats Mom's back awkwardly, almost in the way guys do.

When the orgy of gushing and thank-yous is out of the way, I say flatly, "Thank you. The earrings are beautiful and so are the bangles."

"You're welcome, Tara. I'm glad you like them." Naniji hesitates, then reaches over and squeezes my hand.

Her hand is surprisingly soft, yet firm. It's as though she's saying *I know* and also *It's okay*.

Somehow, that just makes me madder.

Formidable is right.

CHAPTER
12

"You're nuts, Tara," says Erin. "She gives you pearl earrings and you see that as being subversive? And why the heck aren't you wearing them? I want to see them. And your bangles."

I sigh. We're in her room, sprawled on her bed. Erin's room is a total pigsty as usual—clothes everywhere, crusts of bread with rainbow shades of mold—but I had to get away from my house.

"You just don't understand. She's so . . . so . . . it's like she's taken us over. You should see Mom. She's the most nauseating mixture of Marmee-Smarmy and Martha Stewart."

Erin lets out a crack of laughter. "But it's always different when you have visitors. It doesn't matter who it is, you have to adjust. It's the same here, when my grandmother visits, or Mom's sisters."

"Yeah, but—"

"Listen to your *yeah but, yeah but*. You're weird, Tara Mehta. If anyone gave me pearl earrings, they could take over my home anytime."

"But it doesn't feel like home. Everyone's so *formal*. Like we're on *show*. It's *such* a sham." Oh God, I'm italicizing like Mom.

"It won't last long," says Erin soothingly. "Everything'll get back to normal in a day or two. Trust me, the bubble will burst."

I shake my head. "You don't know. You haven't met her."

When I finally go back home, late in the afternoon, Mom, Dad, Maya, and Nina are together in the living room. Still the perfect little magazine family, kids with shiny scrubbed faces—it's like being trapped in one of those fun-house mirrors where everything is distorted.

"Tara," calls Mom, in her most sickening Marmee tone. "Come and join us."

"I've got homework." I head towards my room.

Mom catches up with me near the top of the stairs. "Tara, what is the matter with you?" she whispers.

"Me? What's the matter with *you*?"

Mom raises her eyebrows. "And what exactly do you mean by that?"

"All this, this fake, polite stuff. What're you trying to do? Be the perfect, goody-goody *Indian* daughter-in-law?"

Mom's eyes flash fury. "I am *merely* trying to make her feel welcome, which, apparently, is more than *you* are."

"Hey, I'm not a hypocrite like you."

"It is not hypocrisy to be hospitable. If we all behaved like you, she'd leave in a day."

"Isn't that what you really want?"

"No, it is not."

I laugh. "Yeah, right. That's such a lie. Everything about you is such a lie."

Mom grinds out the words: "It seems my concerns about confiding in you were entirely justified."

"Oh, please." I almost spit. "I'm not influenced by anything *you've* said. If you weren't being so—"

Mom's lips disappear. "She is your father's mother, and if you had *one* iota of concern for anyone else, you'd stop behaving like a spoiled brat and try to make her feel at home."

My face flames. "I don't care if she feels at home—*I* don't feel at home." I run up to my room and bang my door shut.

Loser, loser, loser. All this time I've been supporting her, soothing her, and now she's sold out to the enemy. We're supposed to be united against *her*—the outsider.

At dinnertime, they send Nina up. She smiles at me sympathetically and rubs my arm. "Mom and Dad said you have to come down." Then, tentatively, "What's wrong, Tara?"

I shake my head in disbelief. "Only *you* would have to ask."

Nina's smile fades. "What d'you mean?"

"You and all that . . . gushy-wushy stuff with Naniji; you're so—"

Nina's eyes slit. "Get a life, Tara." She flounces off.

Fine. Who needs her? I head downstairs, humming nonchalantly. I barely glance at Dad, who's helping Mom dish up. I avoid all eye contact with Mom.

Dinner's in the dining room, of course. The best crystal and china, not to mention manners. Even the food is perfect. Indian—everything separate. I never thought I would be, but I'm actually nostalgic for Mom's one-pot *bhaji*—at least it's familiar.

"What a lovely meal, Rohini, Raj. Your *pullao* is delicious, Raj. I didn't know you could cook so well."

Ha! So Dad helped this time—I knew Mom couldn't keep up the traditional thing for long.

Dad shifts uncomfortably. "Well, here, with no servants, we try and share the work, so . . ."

"Of course," says Naniji, a shade too forcefully.

Mom's smile is fixed.

As Naniji gathers a forkful of food, Dad says, "Please, Mummyji, use your hand if you prefer."

There's a sudden pause.

"Yes," says Mom creamily. "No need to be formal."

The cutlery thing. Good!

"No, this is fine." Naniji smiles. "This is how you live, and when in Rome, you know."

Mom's face is carefully neutral, but is she turning red?

"What's Rome got to do with it?" asks Nina.

"It's an expression," says Naniji. "It's actually *When in Rome, do as the Romans do.* Meaning you adapt to your hosts."

Dad glances uneasily at her, then at Mom.

There's a brief silence, then Naniji repeats, "This is really delicious, Rohini."

"Thank you," says Mom.

Naniji turns to me. "So—how did you get along with your homework, Tara?"

"Fine, thank you."

She continues determinedly. "Do you normally get a lot?"

"Sometimes." Hey, I can be just as determined.

Mom and Dad fling eye-darts at me, but Naniji just starts talking to them about people Dad knew in New Delhi. Nina and Maya chip in with questions.

I concentrate on my plate.

Then Naniji slips into Hindi, talking to Dad.

I see how Mom's body tenses.

Naniji looks at us. Another fake smile. "I know the girls don't speak Hindi, but do they understand any?"

Yes! Showdown!

Dad says hastily, "No, no, they don't. . . ."

Mom's tone is pleasant, but there's a hint of iron under satin. "No, the girls are all in French Immersion, and Tara is considering Spanish, so it seems that their plates are pretty full."

Naniji's face is expressionless. "Of course. After all, where would they use Hindi? And your parents didn't speak Hindi to you when you were growing up. . . ." A slight pause before she continues, unconvincingly, "Not that it matters. . . ."

Blood rushes to my face. Gabby and Gampy aren't perfect, but I love them, and, okay, Mom's a pain, and I'm mad at her, but . . .

Mom flashes back sweetly, "No. My parents wanted our English as strong as possible, especially once we were living abroad."

"Of course," says Naniji.

Mom glances at Dad. It's a blatant nudge.

He blinks and clears his throat. "Yes, it's perfectly natural."

The air's thick with things unsaid. And, I'm guessing, things that once *were* said.

Then Nina pipes up. "Say, Naniji, I'd like to learn Hindi. What's Hindi for *fart*?"

I want to stand up and cheer. Yes! Nina's back to normal.

"Nina!" says Mom in a properly horrified tone, as though we *never* utter the word, much less do it.

"That's not funny," snaps Dad.

Naniji says, "I think it's preferable to learn words in context, Nina, don't you?" She doesn't seem shocked, but nor does she have even a glimmer of the laughter Gabby and Gampy have at Nina's BFT.

Nina subsides, half grinning, half squashed.

"Prefra . . . Preferrra. What's that word, Naniji?" asks Maya.

"Preferable." When Naniji looks at Maya, the smile is always genuine. "It means *better*."

Maya tilts her head to one side and thinks. Then says triumphantly, "It's a better word for *better*. *Preff*-rable."

Naniji turns to Nina. "If you really want to learn Hindi, I'll be very glad to teach you. That is, if your mother and father don't mind."

Nina grins sheepishly and shrugs.

"Mind?" Mom's voice rises at least two octaves. "Certainly not. Why would we?"

The dinner limps along to the end.

Naniji gets up. "Now, Raj, Rohini, I insist on helping clear up. I'm also used to doing things, you know."

"I thought you had lots of servants," says Nina.

"Yes, I do have some, but these days in India, it's hard to get good ones, so I've learned to take care of myself. And I don't want your parents to wear themselves out for me."

"No, Mummyji," says Dad. "Please, sit. I'm clearing. You just got here."

Naniji says, "Poor boy, you work all week, now you're waiting on your mother."

Mom flushes scarlet, and Dad says quickly, "Rohini works, too, you know, so . . ."

"Of course, of course, I didn't mean . . ." says Naniji. "With Rohini working as well, it must be hard. Why don't you let me do some cooking? Can I cook for you on week-days?"

"Oh, it really isn't necessary," says Mom hurriedly.

"I didn't mean . . ." says Dad.

"Raj, please. Don't treat me like a guest."

I almost snort out loud. Bit late for that.

"Mummyji," says Dad, "this is your holiday."

"Yes, and it's already a break from my familiar routine. At home I sit on a few volunteer boards which take up a bit of my time, but here I have nothing. Of course, I don't mean to interfere, but if I can help, it would give me pleasure."

I see the war in Mom's eyes—primitive territoriality versus practicality.

Dad looks at Mom, then says, "Well, Mummyji, if you insist."

Oh great! Now she's taking over the cooking, too.

"I'm a plain cook." Naniji smiles. "I'm afraid I don't make fancy things like your mummyji."

"Preff-ra-ble," sings Maya.

"I'm sure your naniji's cooking is preferable to mine," intones Mom.

I can't take it anymore, I just *can't*. I have to burst this bubble, inject a dose of reality.

I push my chair back. "Excuse me, please."

"We haven't had dessert yet, Tara," says Mom. She's still mad, looking through me.

I feel like saying, *Who needs dessert? I've already over-dosed on sweetness.* But I say politely, "I'm afraid I don't want any. I have a phone call to make, and it's getting late." Please let them ask who I'm calling.

"Who do you have to call that can't wait till tomorrow?" asks Dad.

Yes!

"Jeff. I promised I'd show him around this weekend." I turn to Naniji. "Jeff's my . . ." I pause deliberately. ". . . friend."

Naniji's eyebrows rise, then fall again. She keeps her face carefully neutral, but her eyes swivel to Mom and Dad.

Mom and Dad don't even glance at Naniji, but I know what's darting through their panic-stricken minds—what's Naniji going to think of *that*? Do good little Indian girls have boyfriends?

Flash! Exposed!

"Tara," says Dad, "I don't know if you should be making plans . . ." He looks quickly at Naniji.

Naniji lifts both hands. "Please. I want everyone to continue as usual. You have your lives and your way of doing things, and times have changed now."

I look straight at Naniji and smile.

Okay, so she's avoided the showdown this time.

But sooner or later, the gloves will have to come off.

CHAPTER
13

I have it all arranged that I'll spend the day with Jeff, showing him around the Byward Market and a few other places. But Dad corners me after breakfast with the glad tidings that I have to be back by one—he's planned a *family outing* to Gatineau Park, and *it's not up for discussion*.

I'm furious, but when Dad acts the heavy, there's nothing I can do. I know he and Mom cooked this up to get back at me for yesterday.

I meet Jeff near the canal, by First Street, as we'd arranged.

"What's with you?" asks Jeff, as we walk along the canal. "You look kinda . . ." He peers at me. "You're not mad at me, are you?"

"No. It's my stupid parents. I have to be back by one."

"Hey, we still have lots of time, it's only ten-thirty. Come on, let's enjoy what we've got." He shakes my shoulder. "Och, she's in a foul wee mood."

"Jeff!" I thump him.

Then we're both laughing and talking. I point out the sights as we head towards the market. The canal isn't that impressive this time of year; they've just lowered the water level. I tell him how great it is to skate on in the winter, when it freezes.

We go up the spiral stairs onto Wellington Street, and cross over. We peer over the gray stone wall by the Château Laurier at the row of locks down to the river. I point out the curving Museum of Civilization on the other side. I just love that view—it's still amazing, even though the locks are dry.

We head into the market, squeezing past the throngs. There are stalls piled with pumpkins, cabbages, broccoli. We always come here to buy the biggest pumpkins for Halloween.

I take Jeff around to where the crafts are set up. I love the stall with the bright weavings and the little worry dolls from Guatemala. We stop and watch the last of the buskers, then get fries and a drink. Jeff wants to pay, which sort of makes me turn red, but I insist on paying half. I feel relaxed and happy. It's so great being here with Jeff—Mom and Dad are just interested in vegetables.

Then Jeff looks at his watch. "It's twelve-ten. We'd better head home."

My shoulders tense.

"What's the hurry?" It's about a forty-minute walk, taking it easy. I plan on being about ten minutes late—not enough to get into real trouble, just enough to show them who's boss. Gatineau Park. Give me a break!

Jeff nudges me. "What's the matter?"

"Nothing. I just don't want to go back yet."

"Hey, I didn't think I'd see you at all this weekend. When my grandfather visits I'm expected to hang around. Mind you, I want to."

"Yeah, well, I just *had* to get out of there."

Jeff looks puzzled.

I sigh. Erin didn't understand; Jeff probably won't, either, he thinks his grandfather is terrific.

"What's eating you, Tara?"

"Nothing. It's just she's . . ." How do I describe the exaggerated politeness, the distortion—becoming an *Indian* family?

All of a sudden it hits me. Brainwave. Why didn't I think of it before? Yes! It's *way* better than being late.

I say brightly, "Okay, so let's go back. We can hang around my house."

Jeff frowns. "Won't your family mind? Your grandmother just got here."

"Of course not. Come on, she'd love to meet you. Hey, move it, or we won't have time."

"You sure about this?"

"Yeah, yeah, I'm sure. Down here, it's the quickest way."

I am a genius! Naniji'll probably have a cow. Mom and Dad'll have two cows.

I lengthen my stride and we get back at twenty to one. Jeff hesitates as I start up the driveway.

"Hey, look, I don't know if—"

"Oh, Jeff, stop being such a wuss. My life isn't going to stop just because she's here. Anyway, Mom's pining to hear your Scottish accent."

Jeff grins and slowly follows me inside.

Voices from the kitchen. My heart beats faster as I tug Jeff along by the sleeve. Everyone's sitting around the kitchen table.

"Hi, I'm back." I keep my hand on Jeff's arm long enough for all to see.

Mom turns. "Oh, you're early, Tara, good. . . ." Then she sees Jeff. There's only the tiniest pause before she says in her most mature *I-never-do-accents* voice, "Hello, Jeff, nice to see you again."

Nina smirks at me, but I ignore her.

"Hi, Jeff," shouts Maya.

Dad has a dead-codfish smile. Beautiful, just beautiful!

"Jeff, this is my grandmother." How's she taking it?

Her eyes swivel from Jeff to me, to Mom and Dad, then back to Jeff. "Hello, Jeff. It's a pleasure to meet you." She shakes his hand. Smooth. A gracious smile.

No horror or dismay.

Damn.

"Jeff, see the earrings Naniji gave me? And my bangles?" says Maya.

Jeff smiles. "They're lovely, Maya."

"No, they're not lovely," says Maya, twisting her bangles around and around. "They're ex-*quis*-ite."

"Yes, they're exquisite, Maya." We just stand there for a few seconds, no one saying anything.

Jeff fidgets. "Well, I guess I'd better get going."

"Hey, don't be silly," I say, too loudly. "Let's go hang out in my room."

And I get Naniji with that one—she twitches visibly. Jeff turns fiery red.

Mom says hurriedly, "No, no. Join us."

Dad pulls out a couple of chairs and insists, "Please."

"Come on, Jeff." I sit down next to him.

Naniji breaks the silence. "So where did you two go this morning?"

"Er, Tara showed me around the Byward Market."

"We'll have to take you there sometime, Mummyji," says Dad. "It's one of the landmarks of Ottawa."

"I'd like that." Naniji smiles blandly.

Another pause.

Mom and Naniji start to speak at once.

"After you, Mummyji," says Mom.

"I was just going to ask Jeff what kind of market it is."

Jeff says, "I don't know . . . a regular market, I guess."

Mom says, "Oh, it's not like markets in India, it's a mixture of fruits and vegetables, and some crafts, too. A lot of touristy stuff." She rushes on, "In India, you see, there are markets for different things—isn't that right, Mummyji?"

"Yes, in Dilli we have a fish market, another one for vegetables, even one for scrap and junk."

"Hey, cool," says Nina.

Naniji smiles. "Yes, and one called Chor Bazaar, which means 'thieves' market.' Of course, they aren't all thieves; it's just things are cheap there, and people say the goods are stolen. You have to watch out for pickpockets."

"Wow!" says Nina. "I'd really like to go there sometime."

She's such a suck-up!

"Me, too," says Maya.

Naniji's face is wooden.

"Hey, how come we've never been there?" asks Nina disgruntedly.

Drop-dead silence.

Dad says, "Well, you know, the cost for five people . . ."

Mom says, "Of course, India is a fascinating country, but for anyone brought up in the west, it is a culture shock. One has to be careful; the things one takes for granted here, like transportation, safety, and so forth—well, they're different in India."

Naniji flushes. "Millions of people manage to live there."

"Exactly. Millions and millions," says Mom with a smile.

Dad charges in, "The problem is the girls' schools—they don't have long enough breaks over Christmas, and the summers are too hot in India. But maybe sometime . . ."

Naniji looks like she's trying to ignore a bad smell.

Normy waddles into the room, purrs, and arches against Jeff. He bends down and picks her up, like he's relieved to be doing something.

Naniji gathers herself and says, "I can see you like animals, Jeff. Do you have a cat of your own?"

"No, er, I don't. My father has allergies, but, yeah, I love animals." Pause. "Er, do you have pets?"

"No. My husband and I used to have a dog, but she died ages ago."

Jeff tickles Normy, then puts her down gently. He gets up with an air of finality. "I really have to go now. Nice to see you again, Ms. Mehta. And you too, Mr. Mehta. It was nice to meet you, er, Ms. Mehta."

"Bye, Jeff," shouts Maya.

I walk Jeff down the driveway. He's quiet.

"So—see ya tomorrow in school, Jeff."

"Yeah, sure." He doesn't look at me.

I dig him with my elbow, say overheartily, "Hey, what's with you?"

He lets out a huge breath. "In there. Whoa! It was kind of . . ."

"What?"

"I don't know—charged."

"Yeah. Wasn't it just." I grin.

Jeff turns to look at me. "Did you . . . ?" His eyes narrow.

My smile fades. "What?"

"You knew. That, that—it was going to be like . . ."

"What?" It sounds shrill even to me.

Jeff's face is sort of pinched.

"I just wanted you to meet my grandmother," I say, not very convincingly.

"Uh-huh. That would explain the bit about hanging out in your room."

I bite my lip.

Jeff hesitates, then says slowly, "I don't know what your game was, Tara, but it didn't feel too great."

"Hey, come on, don't spaz, I was just . . ."

"Yeah, whatever. Hope you had fun. Bye, Tara." He takes off. He doesn't look back.

My head buzzes.

As I go inside, Mom calls out, coldly, "Tara?" She knows what bringing Jeff here was about. "We're leaving in half an hour. Please wear your sneakers. We'll be walking around some trails."

I grab the cordless phone from the hall table and go upstairs to my room. What on earth happened with Jeff? I mean, *what* happened?

I call Erin and tell her about it.

There's a long silence, then she says, "Oh boy."

"Yeah, I didn't think he'd freak."

"You didn't think he'd . . ." She starts to laugh.

"What?"

"Hey, come on, it was kind of . . ."

"*What?*" I know I sound defensive, but I can't help it.

"Look, Tara . . . it was kind of mean. Think about it. If you were at his house . . ."

"Well, I think he overreacted. Big-time."

Erin murmurs, "Pigheaded, pigheaded!"

"Oh, shut up, Erin."

"Well, what did you expect him to do?"

"Whaddya mean, what did I expect?"

"Whaddya mean, whaddo I mean? Stop with the stupid comedy routine."

I sputter, "I just . . . I never thought he'd . . ."

Erin says dryly, "What? Catch on?"

"No-oo." I sigh heavily. "It's just, *he's* the one who loves to hang out with my family."

"Okay, she doesn't want to face it!"

"Oh, piss off, Erin." This time my voice is sharp.

"Piss off yourself." She's starting to sound annoyed. "Don't take your guilt out on me."

"I don't feel guilty. Why should I? And who the hell's side are you on, anyway?"

"Look, it's not about sides. We're supposed to be straight

with each other, and you're the one giving me attitude, so why the hell should I—"

"Thanks, Erin. For being so *understanding*. Thanks a million." I press the *end* button and fling the phone on my bed.

My hands are trembling. It's just from gripping the phone so hard, that's all.

CHAPTER
14

I stare fixedly out the window as we drive to Gatineau Park. No one bothers to talk to me, except Nina. I snap at her, and Mom and Dad turn around and glare at me; but when Nina says, "Jeez, some grouch," no one says anything to her.

When we pull into the Lake Mulvihill parking lot, I jump out, chin in the air. I stride ahead on the trail, savagely kicking piles of leaves, while they follow behind in a happy little bunch, gushing about the *wonderful, beautiful* colors.

It's the crappiest afternoon. I keep to myself as much as I can, and as soon as we get back home, I disappear into my room, with homework as an excuse.

But I stare at the same math problem for nearly an hour. Should I call Erin?

I don't.

Nobody bothers to talk to me at dinnertime, not even

Nina. I eat quickly, then excuse myself. I try my math again, give up, and play my violin for a bit—funny, I'm so used to playing, it's actually a release.

At bedtime, Mom knocks on my door before coming in. "Tara-My-Stara." She sighs. "Do stop feeling sorry for yourself, love. It isn't so bad, is it?" She touches my cheek briefly. "You always were a fierce and stubborn little thing."

I scorch her with my glare.

When I wake up the next morning, I feel tired and unhappy and—lost? I shake myself. Of course I don't feel lost. I dress quickly and bring a bowl of cereal up to my room.

I pack my bag for school and hang around, waiting for Erin. I leave as late as I can, but she still doesn't come. Guess she needs more time to cool off.

As I open the front door, Mom stops me and wraps her arms around me. She says awkwardly, "I'm sorry I snapped at you the other day, love."

My throat tightens. I manage, "It's okay, I'm sorry, too."

Mom's hand smooths my back. "Want to talk about it?"

I shake my head. "Nah, I've got to get going."

Mom sighs. "All right, kiddo. Have a good day." As I go down the driveway, she calls out, "By the way, I may be late getting home today, okay?"

I nod and stride towards school. Maybe I'll see Erin at the lockers. But there's barely time to get my stuff before the bell goes, and still no Erin. Or Jeff. I don't have any classes with Erin today, but I'll see her at lunchtime, and there's history with Jeff.

I smile hard as I join the crowd at lunchtime. Maybe I'll get Erin out for a walk, and we'll . . . get back to normal. Everyone's there, Nadia, Louise, everyone—except Erin. My stomach sinks. It wasn't that bad a fight—Erin's got a temper, okay, we both have, but we always make up. Then Nadia says something about Erin helping Ms. Gelder with the drama props, but—what if she's avoiding me?

My head's starting to throb by the time I go to my history class. I get there early and sit up front. I don't mean to watch, but my eyes keep swiveling towards the door. But Jeff still isn't there by the time Tolly arrives. I'm not sure if I'm more relieved or disappointed.

Tolly perches up front in his usual storklike posture, one leg on the chair, his bushy eyebrows flying. He drones on and on about how history changes depending on who is telling it, and he reminds us about the assignment he gave us last week.

We're supposed to write an account of a personal life, tied to a moment of historical significance. It's so dumb—ask our parents what they were doing when Trudeau became prime minister, or when JFK was assassinated, or where our grandparents were during the war. *Any event in world history, not just Canadian. Talk to family members. They know about living history.* He looks at Trev, whose family had to leave Uganda. Oh, please. It's always about kids who look different, isn't it?

Naturally, the way my day's going, I get stuck to present on the first day, along with Guy and a few others. It's due Thursday, for God's sake—that's just three days away; what the heck am I going to do?

At the end of the day, when I get to my locker, there's no sign of Erin. Okay, so she's often late, but there's no way I'm waiting around like I did this morning. Obviously, Erin is way less mature than I thought. My head hurts and, boy, am I sick of smiling.

I walk home fast. As I turn down my driveway, I smell Indian food. Erin would shove her way in, of course, if she was here. Yeah, well, her loss.

I open the front door.

Naniji comes out of the kitchen. The smooth smile, tidy, contained. And wary. "Hello, Tara," she says, stiffly. "How was school?"

"Fine, thanks. Where's Mom?"

"She's still at work. She said this morning that she'd be late."

I forgot.

Naniji says, "I made a small after-school snack. Samosas. Come and have some."

Damn. I love samosas.

Maya comes running to hug me. "Hi, Tara. The samosas are dee-licious." At least *somebody* cares. I hug her back.

Naniji says, "Come into the kitchen, there's plenty. I made lots, thinking you might bring some friends home."

My back prickles. I don't need her inviting me to sit in my own kitchen. "I'm not hungry, thank you. Anyway, I'd better do my homework."

"My, you certainly are conscientious," says Naniji.

I look at her sharply, then shrug and head upstairs.

"Hi, Tara," calls Nina as I'm halfway up. "The samosas are really great."

I smile weakly, shut my door behind me, and flop onto the bed. Alone at last. Deep breaths. I am not going to cry. Everything's fine, just *fine*.

It's just, the house feels weird without Mom. Too quiet. And, okay, lately I've had to babysit Maya way too often, and it's not like I love it or anything, but—*I'm* supposed to be in charge when Mom's not around, not *her*. And why's Mom still at work? She said she could work her own hours, and from home. I bet she's avoiding Naniji.

The phone rings.

"Tara," Nina bellows. "It's for you. I'll bring it up."

I sit up as Nina comes in and hands me the cordless phone.

"Thanks," I say gruffly.

"You're welcome." Nina hesitates, then reaches out and pats my arm.

My throat tightens and I hug her before she runs downstairs.

I put the receiver to my ear. "Hello?"

"Hi, it's me." Erin's voice is uncertain.

"Oh, hi."

"Remember me?"

"Yeah."

"So how're you doing?"

"Okay. Fine." I tuck my hair behind my ear.

A long pause. Erin sighs. "What the hell's gotten into you, Tar?"

"Nothing."

"Hello. This is me, your best friend. Remember? Talk to me."

"I didn't think you'd want to hear my problems." I blink my eyes hard.

"Boy, are you ever an idiot!" She's half laughing.

"Thanks a lot."

"You're welcome. You asked for it."

"Thanks a lot again."

"You're welcome again, dummy."

"Dummy to you, too."

"Yeah, well, double dummy to you."

We both shout together, "Dummy to the power of infinity."

The knot in my chest is starting to loosen.

Erin says, "So, dummy to the power of infinity, how come you didn't wait for me after school?"

"How come you didn't come by this morning?"

"For God's sake, I had band practice—it's Monday."

"Oh! I forgot!"

Erin clicks her tongue. "Like I said, double dummy to the power of infinity."

The knot is almost all gone.

I hesitate, then say, "What about lunchtime? Did you really have to help Ms. Gelder, or—"

"Of course I was helping her! You didn't think . . . ?"

"Okay, okay! Just checking."

Erin sighs dramatically. Then casually, she says, "By the way, I thought I smelled something gooood as I walked past your house. What did your mother make this time?" She makes a slurping noise.

I let out a crack of laughter. "Erin, you pig!"

She's laughing, too. "That's me." Her tone becomes pleading. "So what is it?"

"It's the grandmother. Samosas."

"Samosas!" moans Erin.

"Okay, okay, come on over."

"You sure? Shouldn't you ask her?"

"Look, it's my house. And do you, or do you not, want samosas?"

"Hey, don't get all bent out of shape. I'm coming. Love ya." She makes a kissing noise and hangs up.

I run downstairs, then stop outside the kitchen.

I take a deep breath and pop my head around the door. "I just want you to know, I have a friend coming over." My voice is carefully polite, but there's no trace of asking in it.

Naniji looks up and smiles. No, beams. A tidy, well-contained beam, but still a beam. "Of course."

"Can I have my friends over, too?" pipes up Nina.

"Sure." I flush, look defiantly at Naniji.

"Of course," says Naniji quickly. "Whatever your parents normally let you do."

Nina's eyes glow. "They let me have anyone over."

"Then it's fine with me." Naniji smiles.

"Thanks, Naniji." Nina jumps up. "I'll go call them."

"I've had *two* samosas, Tara," says Maya.

I give her a big kiss, then run outside to wait for Erin. As I reach the bottom of the driveway, she comes tearing up. We hug each other.

"I'm sorry," I wail. "I was such an idiot."

"Aww! I'm sorry, too," says Erin.

I squeeze her hard. "But it was more my fault."

Erin pokes me. "Okay, I'll give you that."

Then we're inside, and Naniji is shaking hands with Erin and ushering us into the kitchen.

There's a big plateful of samosas on the table, along with some green chutney.

This feels so strange. Why is Erin standing around, instead of diving in?

Naniji indicates the plate. "Please."

As Erin takes a samosa, I slowly reach for one, too. Am I caving in?

"Oh, this is *fabulous*," breathes Erin. She looks like she's having a spiritual experience.

"It's good," I say, awkwardly. There are potatoes and peas and some spice—cumin, I think—that's just right. And the green chutney is minty and garlicky and pretty terrific.

"Fabulous," says Maya, watching Erin with complete and utter fascination. She half closes her eyes and tilts her head back, just like Erin.

I laugh.

"I'm so glad," says Naniji. She looks genuinely pleased— as Mom does when we like something she's cooked.

"You'll have to tell me the kinds of after-school snacks you like, so I can make them."

I look sharply at her. How long is she staying, anyway? And is Mom going to work late every night while she's here?

Nina comes running into the kitchen. "I have a bunch of kids coming over, okay, Naniji?"

"Of course." Another beam.

I grab my chance.

"Come on, Erin, let's go to my room." I take a small plateful of samosas and we head upstairs. Erin smiles widely at Naniji and says thank you.

"Hey, she's not that bad," says Erin after I shut my door. "Kind of stiff, maybe, a bit old-worldish, but basically okay."

I ruffle Erin's wiry hair. "Yeah, well, you'd sell your soul for samosas."

Erin thwacks me, but picks up another samosa. "Come on, admit it, what's to hate?"

I sigh. "Okay, okay, I don't know. I guess I don't actually *hate* her—but what's to like? She may not be a total monster, but . . ."

"Big of you." Erin grins.

"Hey, I'm not a stomach like you—a few samosas aren't going to win me over like . . . like a heathen converted to the light."

Erin bursts out laughing.

I start laughing, too.

CHAPTER
15

After Erin leaves I take out the pearl earrings. I hesitate, then try them on. They are exquisite, as Maya says—I guess it doesn't hurt to leave them on. I make a face at my reflection, then pop on my gracious smile.

When I go down, Mom, Dad, and Naniji are yakking away in the kitchen, while Naniji stirs something on the stove. So she's cooking dinner, too.

Naniji notices right away. "Thank you for wearing the earrings, Tara. They look beautiful on you."

I flush. She makes it sound like I've done her the favor.

Mom kisses me and strokes my cheek. "Lovely, sweetie," she says.

Even Dad smiles approvingly. I feel a pinprick of irritation, but I can't be bothered to react.

When we sit down to eat—in the kitchen, because Naniji insists we carry on as normal—the dinner is perfect. A chick-pea curry, rice, a cauliflower-and-potato *bhaji*, and a green-bean *bhaji*. All separate. And *chapatis*. Actual *chapatis*, perfectly round. Mom never makes them, because they're too much work.

"Oh, this is delicious," says Dad, visibly relaxing. "Sour chick-peas—my favorite when I was little." He takes a huge portion.

Naniji glows. "See, I remembered. I remember everything."

Mom says, "How nice. We *both* do so appreciate you cooking."

Did she say that a shade too brightly, or am I just being paranoid?

"My pleasure," Naniji says, smiling.

"Pleashure," says Maya, eyes fixed on Naniji.

The chick-pea curry is good—it has surprising chunks of tomatoes and onion in it, but, unlike the stuff Mom flings in, they actually belong there.

Nina raves on and on about it, and I feel my body relax as Naniji's food works its magic on me. Whaddya know, I've gone mellow. Naniji must've put something in the food. Hash. Ha! I'll have to tell Mom later. But perhaps, the way she is now, she wouldn't find it funny.

I catch something Naniji is saying.

". . . he interviewed me about it."

Dad says, "I'm glad. Papaji's contribution shouldn't be forgotten. Or yours." He glances uneasily at Mom, who is smiling stiffly.

What? What did I miss?

Naniji tears a portion of *chapati* and wraps it around some cauliflower. I wonder if Mom's noticed that Naniji is now eating with her hands.

"I don't know if we need yet another book about the Independence struggle, but I think this one is more personal history rather than all the facts. You know . . ." She says something to Dad in Hindi, then catches herself, looks at Mom, and says in English, "All the little-little things that don't make the textbooks, the costs to personal life."

Mom's jaw tightens. She carefully loads her fork with rice.

Nina pipes up, "My grandfather's going to be in a book? And you? Cool. What kinds of things did you do? I know he went to jail and stuff, but . . ." She glances at me, then away.

I stifle my grin and spear some beans.

Maya chips in, "He was a hero. Dad said."

Naniji sits straighter. "Yes, his whole family suffered terribly, but they followed Gandhiji's ideals, even when it wasn't convenient. Three years he spent in jail. Three. And his father, your great-grandfather, he was in and out of jail—nine years in total!"

One little, two little, do I hear three little jailbirds? I shove a large forkful of food into my mouth to choke down my laughter.

"Why? What was the reason?" Nina blurts out.

Naniji's voice is startled. "Don't they know?"

Dad swallows hastily. "Yes, yes, of course they do. I've told them about the Independence movement, and Papaji being jailed. But they don't know all the specifics, maybe."

"I see." Naniji's lips are tight.

Here she goes again!

Nina says, "Dad's hopeless with details, Naniji." She puts down her fork. "Why was my grandfather arrested?"

"Civil disobedience." Naniji's face is calm, proud. I fleetingly remember Mom saying something about the high moral ground. "The laws were terrible, unjust—the whole British rule, their presence in our country, it was wrong. And Gandhiji taught us that the right thing to do with injustice was to oppose it." Naniji raises her eyebrow disdainfully. "So we boycotted British goods, and we refused to obey their unjust laws. Tilak, your grandfather, was arrested for picketing a shop carrying foreign cloth from England."

I stop, fork midway to mouth.

"Why foreign cloth?" asks Nina.

For once I'm glad she asks. I kind of want to know, too, but there's no way I'm acting all interested.

Dad chips in, "Because it took away work from Indian spinners and weavers, the cottage industries, and the profits ended up in England."

I look from Dad to Naniji. She's his mother—they don't look anything alike, but they have this shared history. I tear off a piece of *chapati* and chew it slowly.

"That's right," says Naniji. "Before the British rule, we used to export textiles."

Mom says deliberately, as though reciting a lesson, "Yes, I remember my father saying that the British didn't come to India because it was poor, but because it was fabulously wealthy."

There's a funny look in Naniji's eyes—sort of surprised, but guarded. Mom flushes.

"Exactly," says Naniji. "But they completely bled us dry. They sent our cotton over to England, to make work for their people, and brought it back to sell at huge profits." Naniji squares her shoulders. "So we boycotted all foreign goods."

Her face—it's like she's fully awake for the first time since she got here.

"And the freedom fighters, we wore plain white *khadi*—homespun cotton, hand-woven. It was rough, but we refused to wear the imported. And we protested nonviolently—Gandhiji was adamant about it. That was the way of a Satyagrahi."

"What?" asks Nina.

"The freedom fighters, that's what they were called," says Dad, helping himself to some more chick-peas. He looks so eager, like a kid.

Mom smiles faintly as she fiddles with her napkin ring.

"Yes, it means an upholder of the truth—that's what the fight was about, truth and justice. I remember Tilak, wearing *khadi*, going to join the demonstration, carrying a *Quit India* sign—that was the cry in '42—just *Quit India*."

All I know about 1942 is World War II was going on. I think.

"So why was he arrested?" Nina asks.

Naniji's eyes glitter. "Oh, just for protesting. He and thousands of others. All nonviolent protestors. Even Arjun, my oldest brother. You know what they did, the British? They were on horses, and they charged the protestors. They hit unarmed people with sticks, *lathis*—big, long five-foot sticks, with steel tips—and they aimed for the head, that's what they did. And fired into unarmed crowds. Thousands died, thousands."

There's a shocked silence. Maya's eyes are round.

"For picketing?" I squeak.

"Yes." Naniji's face is grim. "It was a terrible time. All our civil liberties, they were taken away. Gandhiji, all our leaders were arrested, many with no trial."

I lean forward. I can't help it. It's the first genuine conversation we've had since she got here. Even Mom seems reluctantly interested. And we've all stopped eating, even Dad.

Naniji continues, fiercely. "There, in Europe, the British were fighting a war for democracy and freedom, but that didn't apply to India, oh no. And when we protested about the arrests, they cracked down even more. They banned demonstrations, meetings, they closed down newspapers—the police were like licensed thugs, they had full power."

Mom says, "Yes, it was all in the movie *Gandhi*—the curfews, the injustices. A complete disgrace." She adds defensively, "My parents have talked about it, too."

Naniji hesitates, then says, "Yes. I suppose it was hard for everyone."

Dad's shoulders come down.

"But for the Satyagrahis . . ." Naniji shakes her head. "I remember how they used to come, the British soldiers, to Tilak's parents' house. You know"—she turns to us—"your great-grandfather's? They lived next door to us. I remember looking out my bedroom window and seeing the British taking away half the furnishings, and big, big paintings. All confiscated, because his father refused to pay their fines." Her eyes flash. "They faced terrible hardship. But Tilak and his father, they demonstrated anyway."

"Wow!" breathes Nina.

Maya's mouth is full but she's stopped chewing.

Dad says, "Of course, the main reason they locked up Papaji was because he was his father's son."

Naniji's eyes are moist. "He was so badly beaten. Three years he lost. He was just about to start his engineering degree. He was brilliant." Her voice is thick with emotion. "You should have seen him when he came out—he'd lost so much weight. He looked ten years older."

Nina looks soberly at me. I feel kind of squirmy that we laughed about it, but also a bit annoyed at Dad. Why on earth didn't he explain it better?

"Were you engaged to him back then?" asks Nina quietly.

"No, not until later. But he and Arjun were close. In fact, it was because they were so close that some of my family were arrested." She pauses, then jerks out, "On my fourteenth birthday."

"What happened?" I'm a bit surprised I'm asking, but I really want to know.

Naniji takes in a deep breath, as though she's lifting a weight. "I'll tell you some other time."

It strikes me—this small woman is actually my grandmother. I know nothing about her stories. Gabby and Gampy, we've heard so many of theirs: Gampy's days at Cambridge, their honeymoon in Paris. . . .

"Were you involved in the Independence movement, too?"

Naniji looks pleased I've asked. "Yes, I was. After that terrible time in '42."

"Way to go, Naniji," says Nina.

She flushes, smiles suddenly. "I even used to spin *khadi*. I remember how hot and sticky the cotton would be in the worst of the summer, but I did it for Gandhiji."

"You met Mahatma Gandhi, didn't you?" says Mom eagerly. He's one of her heroes. "What was he really like?"

Naniji's face glows. "He was so inspiring! You can't imagine—here was this small man, wearing a *dhoti*—you know, the loincloth—being Indian, and completely routing the British. He wasn't intimidated by those big-shot white sahibs. Do you know, one of his most devoted followers was an English woman, the daughter of an admiral? The British, they were so outraged that one of them could actually support the *natives*." She spits out the word.

It's like a punch in my stomach.

Is *that* what it was like? Mom and Dad have told us bits, but it's always been remote; history—I never *felt* it before. Native. That's how it was here, with the Native Indians, as well as black people. It still is, at times.

Naniji leans forward. "But Gandhiji showed us that we could be proud of ourselves—we weren't just as good as the British, but better, morally." For the first time she isn't filtering her words. Her voice exudes scorn. "We didn't have to shed everything Indian like a dirty skin and become brown sahibs, dressing like them, talking like them—and scrambling and scratching to live in the west."

It takes a few seconds to register. Then Mom sits back, her smile a scar on her face.

Naniji blinks. "Not that there's anything wrong with . . ."

"No, of course not," says Dad. His eyes are angry and pleading at the same time.

A slight pause before Naniji says, "After all, many of our leaders were educated in the west. I went to an English-run school for a while; there wasn't much else, and . . ."

I fumble for something, anything, to mend the silence. I mean, it was just starting to get real. Tolly.

My words spill out: "Naniji, I have to do a project on a personal life during a moment in history. Could I maybe ask you about the Indian Independence movement, you know, things you did, and . . . and use that?" I'm slightly breathless.

Naniji's smile is so brimming with gratitude, it makes me squirm.

"I'd be delighted, Tara."

"Wonderful idea," says Dad. He quickly turns the conversation to safer grounds.

I slowly let out my breath and watch Naniji covertly. I don't know what I feel about her, if I even like her. But one thing's for sure, she's got guts. She isn't a subservient little woman. In many ways, she and Mom are more alike than they realize.

Hey! Maya is like Naniji, and Mom often says Maya and I are alike. . . . Connect the dots.

Naniji sees me staring and smiles. It's so genuine that I smile back spontaneously. Somehow, I can't help it. Anyway, what does it hurt?

CHAPTER
16

Back in my room, I pace up and down, oddly unsettled.

Dad should have been clearer about it—no wonder Mom gets mad at him for being vague, for not talking. But, then, she's always dumping on India. But if Naniji was scornful of . . . it's so convoluted. And stupid. I mean, get over it!

But I held it together today. Me. Whaddya know! Except I'll have to talk to her now. The assignment's due Thursday.

I sigh and start my math homework—pages and pages—then take out my English folder and finish my analysis on a poem by Robert Frost. Slowly, I flip back to my biography on Jeff. I got an A for it.

The look in his eyes when he said *Hope you had fun. Bye, Tara*. Sort of sad, and angry and—I guess I can admit it now—hurt.

Erin and I talked about it over the samosas, and she said that I should definitely try and talk to him. But what if he's still mad at me?

I pull open my top drawer. There it is, the piece of paper with his phone number. My heart thuds. I could call him, remind him about the history assignment. Then what? *I'm sorry, Jeff, that you were uncomfortable; I just didn't think?* Or *Hey, what's up? Want to hang out this weekend?*

I fold the bit of paper over and over. He probably doesn't even like me—I mean, Erin's my friend, she's biased.

I put back the piece of paper and bang the drawer shut. Tomorrow. I have English, so I'll see him for sure, if he's in school. A small voice inside whispers *chicken,* but I squash it. Hey, Erin and I are okay again, and I've reached a precarious truce with Naniji—that's enough for one day. I take out my violin and tuck it under my chin. The solidness is so familiar. Reassuring. I draw the bow across the strings, and it's like the violin's a part of me, just pulling, pulling out music. I play until that hard, edgy feeling goes down.

As Erin and I walk to school together the next morning, she asks, casually, "So—you going to talk to Jeff today?"

I shrug. "I guess, maybe. . . ."

Erin grins. "It's going to be fine, Tara."

I'm trying to keep my dignity, really I am, but before I can stop myself, I'm moaning, "What if he's still mad at me?" I can't believe how whiny I sound.

"Aww! Come here!" Erin puts her arm around me.

At school, Erin and I hang around the lockers and watch out for Jeff, but there's no sign of him. Finally, the bell goes, and I have to get to math. Nadia joins me as I head to class, and on the way we see Guy talking to Tolly. He's asking loudly if there's a limit to how long he can make the history assignment. "I've got a lot of great stuff, Mr. Toller," he says importantly.

Nadia and I poke our fingers in our mouths and make gagging sounds. Tolly, of course, looks all pleased—hey, you can't lay it on thick enough for him. Naniji's face flashes in my head, that look of determination. I'll have to talk to her today. Tolly will love it—a nice display of exotica. I'll probably get an A triple plus!

English is last period. When I get there I look around the classroom. But no Jeff. Maybe he isn't even in school today. I sit near the back, with a couple of empty desks nearby.

Then Ms. Gelder comes in and everyone settles down. Poetry again, for God's sake.

The door creaks open. Jeff.

He glances in my direction, at the empty desk next to me.

I try to smile, but my mouth won't work. By the time I make it, he's turned towards the other empty desk, across the room from me, and I'm smiling like a dummy at the air.

Fine. Who cares? I keep my smile pasted on and act like I'm riveted by Ms. Gelder. I don't hear a word she's saying. From the corner of my left eye, I can see Jeff's blue sweater—staining my vision, spreading. I won't look at him, I won't!

Ms. Gelder's talking about an American poet, Edwin Markham. My ears buzz. It's so dumb, the way teachers tell you what a poem is supposed to mean, as though they can see inside the poet's head.

The blue at the corner of my eye shifts. Jeff's tapping his eraser on the desk.

Ms. Gelder's saying something about an epigram called "Outwitted" as she strides up and down between the desks. I miss the page number, fumble at my book. When Ms. Gelder reaches me, she turns my book to the right page and quirks an eyebrow. "Distracted, are we?"

Blood rushes to my face. I haven't taken my eyes off her, I really haven't.

The blue at the corner of my eye sits back.

Listen, just listen, I tell myself fiercely.

Ms. Gelder begins to recite: "'. . . a circle that shut me out . . .'"

I look down, read:

> *"He drew a circle that shut me out—*
> *Heretic, rebel, a thing to flout*
> *But Love and I had the wit to win:*
> *We drew a circle that took him in."*

Edwin Markham, 1852–1940. I read the lines over and over.

"Tara, are you with us?" asks Ms. Gelder.

My face burns. "Sorry, I . . . I was just looking at the poem and . . ."

Ms. Gelder's face actually lights up.

"Go on."

Jeez, why is she drawing attention to me? I hate speaking out in class. But she's waiting, all eager.

I take in a deep breath and blurt out, "I . . . I was thinking about how artificial it all is, you know, lines and groups and all that . . . that classifying." Great, way to be articulate, Tara.

Ms. Gelder nods intently. "Go on."

Stop it, Tara—show him, show her I'm capable of thinking. I'm surprised at how the words rush out. "Well, I don't like to be told I'm part of this group, or that. It's like everyone's always drawing circles and lines, but no one has the right. I'm me. And everyone's an individual. A group of one."

There's an explosion of voices. "Yeah, right on," and, "You got it!"

But someone calls out, "Isn't that kinda lonely?"

Kate says something about family, and Lynne cries, "What about community? Belonging?"

I'd like to shrink and disappear. But Ms. Gelder is thrilled that we're actually discussing a poem. She says something about how that's the whole point of the poem, to expand our notion of community. Then Jessie says something about how we need to define, to understand the world, how it's only natural. There's a big argument going on. I turn to look at Jessie, then glance quickly at Jeff. He's looking at me.

I flush and turn away. Jeez, I shouldn't have done that. I look at him again, but his eyes are down on his book, his face stiff.

Ms. Gelder tries to get us to elaborate, but I don't hear a word anyone says. The blue at the corner of my eye, *a thing to flout*. Out. He's white, I'm not. I bite my lip. What the hell made me think that?

Then the bell goes and there's the scraping of chairs. Okay, now's my chance. My hands tremble, but I slap on a friendly smile and turn towards Jeff.

He's on his way out. Jessie runs up to him and tugs his sleeve, and they leave together, heads close. Blood rushes to my face. But I keep my grin on as I go down the hallway. I catch glimpses of Jeff and Jessie ahead—they both stop by his locker. I hum lightly as I pass them.

Erin has band. Not that there's anything particular to tell her.

I give myself a good harsh talking-to as I walk home. *Don't be so dumb, Tara.* Good thing I didn't call last night. He's fine with things the way they are. Just fine. And I am, too. She's white, Jessie. Hey, all them honkies like to stick together, don't they? Okay, so that's really crappy and unfair. But next time I see him I won't even look at him. Not that I'm avoiding him or anything; I'll just say hi, like I would to anyone else, be casual. I mean, he's new here, and all he wanted was a friend. We were never anything more than that, anyway.

CHAPTER
17

I fumble for my keys and let myself in.

Quiet in here—Mom must be working at the shelter again. Sure is spending a lot of time there. Away from Naniji.

Nina's in the family room with a few friends, watching a video, and Maya's hanging out with them. I wave. Maya comes running to hug me, then rushes back to her movie. I just want to escape to my room, but Naniji comes from the kitchen and says, "Hello, Tara."

I smile awkwardly. "Hi, Naniji." I think it's the first time I've called her that.

"Your mummyji is still at work. I'm putting together dinner. Do you want a snack?"

I want to go to my room, I need to, but I did that before to get away from her—she'll get the wrong idea. And she's looking so . . . all by herself.

I take a deep breath. "Well, okay, sure." I drop my bag and follow her into the kitchen.

Carrots, celery, and a white dip. Oh. No Indian stuff.

Naniji says, anxiously, "I hope this is all right?"

"Yeah, sure, it's fine." I stick a carrot into the dip and crunch. "Mm. It's good. What is it?"

Naniji beams. "Yogurt. I thought maybe it's good to have something not fried today, no?"

Jeez, shades of Mom.

"Sit. Sit. I'm just chopping some eggplant for the *bhaji* for dinner."

This feels so weird. I glance towards the family room— I wish Nina and her friends were here, it'd be easier. Slowly, I pull the chair back and sit down. I pick up a stick of celery.

Naniji looks at me eagerly and goes back to slicing the eggplant. "I thought I'd have it all ready, but your daddyji took some time off around lunch. We ate at a restaurant on the canal and went for a walk. It ended up being longer than I expected, then I lay down for a bit and lost track of time."

I smile and crunch the celery.

"So, you see, I'm a little late," continues Naniji.

And I do see. I see that anxious look in her eyes and how hard she's trying, and she's so small. I remember everything she said yesterday, demonstrations, wearing homespun—and the way I treated her. She's come all this way, and, okay, I don't like that she scorned Mom or Gabby and Gampy, and I don't want her calling the shots, I've made that clear, but still she's trying.

I get up abruptly. "Why don't I help, Naniji? I often cut things for Mom."

Her delight spears me.

I swallow, flash a smile, and reach for the other chopping board. "What d'you want me to do?"

"Maybe peel some garlic? Four or five cloves?"

"Sure."

For a moment we work in silence, though it isn't entirely awkward. It's good to have something to do, it keeps my mind off—*stop it, Tara, he isn't even here, and Naniji is.* I rub the papery skin off the garlic and search for something to talk about.

Then I remember. "Say, Naniji, can you tell me about your part in the Independence struggle? You know, for my history assignment?"

I can sense her relief, too, that there's some safe ground. "Of course."

I've finished peeling the garlic. "Is there anything else you want me to do?"

"Cut some ginger, maybe? About an inch. And can you chop it fine, with the garlic? I'll start this."

She turns the burner on and pours some canola oil into the frying pan.

I get the ginger from the fridge, break off a piece, and hold it up to her. She nods.

"Now, what do you want me to tell you?"

"I don't know. I guess, well—what kinds of things did you do? You said something about your fourteenth birthday."

She looks quickly at me, then away. "Yes. It was the day the arrests started. August 9, 1942. The beginning of the Quit India movement."

I frown. "Nineteen forty-two? That's when the Independence movement began?"

"Oh no, no, no. It had been going on for years and years, from even the middle of the 1800s and then really strongly from 1919—that was after a terrible massacre of Indians by the British in Amritsar." A pause. "You haven't heard about that?"

I shake my head.

Naniji grunts.

Oh, great. Is she going to get all bent out of shape?

She sees my face and says hastily, "Well, I won't go into that now. There were many struggles, many, but the time I got involved, that was '42. The Quit India movement. Gandhiji, all the leaders, issued a statement calling for the British to quit India, immediately."

"So you weren't involved before?" Somehow I'd seen it as an ongoing thing. I start to chop the ginger and garlic.

Naniji shakes her head. "No, I'm afraid I didn't pay much attention to what was going on. You see, until then, even though my parents were involved, they didn't actually court arrest like Tilak's father. My father was a doctor, and his patients needed him. Also, he was the only breadwinner, and we didn't have money like Tilak's family."

"Court arrest?" I stop cutting.

Naniji throws some black-mustard seed into the frying pan, covers it as the seeds pop, and turns off the burner. "It's what the Satyagrahis did, you know, the freedom fighters—deliberately."

She takes two onions from the basket and starts to peel one. "But my parents supported the cause, too—they were close to Tilak's mother and father, and through them they gave money to families of jailed protestors. Secretly, of course."

"Secretly?"

"Oh yes, you had to—you could be arrested just for that."

"You're kidding."

"No, it's true. That's how bad it was."

I give the ginger and garlic one last going-over with my knife and take one of the onions from her.

Naniji continues, "But me, well, I suppose I was caught up in my own little life. I was so naïve, so naïve. And frivolous, too, I think."

Frivolous? Naniji?

She smiles. "No, really. I was."

"What happened?" I start to peel the onion.

Naniji says grimly, "My fourteenth birthday."

Fourteen. It's just one year younger than I am, two years older than Nina.

Naniji's eyes narrow. "You see, until then, I just accepted it without really thinking—you know, the . . . the values." She blinks rapidly. "How everything British was white and right and our culture just rubbish. It happens when you're constantly put down and it's rubbed into you."

I frown and cut my onion in two. If I'd experienced more Samanthas . . .

"You know, there were clubs Indians couldn't join, and it was all to do with color, nothing else. Even if you were educated in England, lived like them, talked like them, you still couldn't join, because you weren't white. Black, they called us. All Indians were simply black. They were so arrogant, the British, they never looked *at* us, but *through* us, like we were worthless. Even in the school I went to—it was the best English one, for Indians. The whites had their own, of course." She sniffs as her eyes start to water.

I slice the onion slowly.

"I used to get so irritated with my parents, because they were strict about keeping things Indian at home."

"Yeah? Like what?" I can't see Naniji as a teenager bugged by her parents.

"Well . . ." She frowns, then laughs suddenly. "Like nail polish. I used to beg and beg my mother to let me use it, but she never would. I thought it was so, I don't know, sophisticated. Unlike the *mehndi*—you know, henna that's used to make patterns on the hand? I thought everything Indian was so boring and only western ways were glamorous."

"Hey, and *mehndi* is real cool here now!" I grin at her. "What else?"

"Oh, we'd sit on the floor to eat, use metal *thalis*— plates—and eat with our hands. And speak Hindi at home."

Mom and the cutlery flashes in my head.

"And I, well, I was uncomfortable. I'd always reply in English. The only time I spoke Hindi was to the servants who didn't speak English. You see, if my parents hadn't insisted, I wouldn't have known anything about being Indian. At school the only history we learned was their version of it, the wonderful progress they'd brought to India." Her lip curls into a sneer.

"So why did your parents send you there?" I start to cut the onion across.

"You had to know English to get anywhere—they controlled everything. Besides"—Naniji raises a finger—"if you want to defeat your enemy, you need to learn to think like them."

I laugh out loud.

"But those teachers, they made us feel like everything Indian was . . . was . . ." Naniji searches for the right word, then continues, ". . . backwards, primitive. Inferior."

Native. I remember how she said it.

I ask quietly, "Did you feel inferior?"

Naniji flushes. "Yes . . . I suppose so. But I didn't know it then. Or how unjust the system was. Until the arrests." Her jaw tightens. "I remember, the day before my birthday, Arjun and Tilak, they were whispering on the veranda. It was terribly hot. I remember how they stopped talking when I went by. I poked my tongue out at my brother—I thought it was so boring, how serious he was, and Tilak, too. He was seventeen at the time, and I didn't like him at all. Then, that evening, at dinner, Arjun told us what he'd heard from Tilak. Our leaders were issuing a statement calling on Britain to Quit India. Immediately. I'll never forget it. It was like an electric jolt went through the room. Everyone stopped eating. There was just the sound of the ceiling fan whirring. Those words, *Quit India*, so sharp, so decisive." She draws in a deep breath. "Then I, I piped up, *Ma, what about my birthday?*"

Naniji's eyes are faraway. Suddenly, she says loudly, "*Karengae ya marengae.*"

I jump.

Naniji turns to me, and it's like her eyes come back. "*Do or Die.* That was the slogan. We will do or die to get the British to leave; do or die for our freedom."

I take a deep breath.

"Hello, I'm home."

I swing around. Mom's standing at the doorway. I didn't even hear her come in.

CHAPTER
18

Mom says lightly, "This looks cozy."

"Yeah, well, I'm talking to Naniji about the Independence movement—it's for my assignment." I'm annoyed that I'm explaining.

Naniji says quickly, "Yes, yes, she asked me."

Mom raises her eyebrow elegantly. "Of course. I'm sure it's invaluable information."

I almost say something sharp, but there's something vulnerable about her mouth—I go over and give her a kiss.

She squeezes me. "Thanks, pet. Keep on, don't let me stop you."

But it's gone, that easiness. Mom's cut the thread Naniji was spinning for me. I wish Mom would just, I don't know, go up to her room or something.

Naniji turns to Mom. "And how was your day, Rohini?"

"Oh, fine, fine. There's an amazing amount of work, more than I anticipated, which is why I'm late." She glances at the cut eggplant on the counter and says unconvincingly, "Er, I can continue here, with the dinner."

"No, no, it's all right. Tara's helping, you see."

Mom's smile is forced. "How lovely." She fills the kettle with water.

I turn away from Mom and start to chop the onion fiercely. My eyes sting. "Go on, Naniji, you were telling me—your birthday, what happened?"

Naniji sighs. "That's when the mass arrests started. Later we found out that all our leaders had been arrested, every single one. But we didn't know it at the time. All I cared about was having a good birthday. I remember I had a bright-yellow *salwar khameez* for the party, it was new. You know *salwar khameez*?" She indicates her clothes, the long top and baggy pants, then glances quickly at Mom.

Mom looks slightly offended.

"Go on, Naniji," I urge.

"So—I had several friends coming over. I remember how my mother was fussing around, distracted. She must have known, poor woman, what was happening; she was close to Tilak's mother. But she was determined I would have a special day. Tilak, his mother, their whole family were invited, too, but I didn't care if they came. There were no girls my age in his family, and I thought Tilak was so stern and dull."

"Who was so dull?" Nina comes in with Maya. Her friends must have left—I never heard them, either.

Maya jumps onto Mom's lap and plants a noisy kiss. Nina sits at the table and repeats, "Who was so dull? What're you talking about?"

"Will you be quiet?" I say irritably. "Naniji's telling me about what happened to her during the . . . the freedom struggle. It's for my assignment, so *shush*."

Mom raises her eyebrows at me.

Nina glowers. "Well, I want to hear, too. I mean, I'm interested."

The kettle shrieks and Mom gets up to pour water into the teapot.

I keep chopping the onion as Naniji goes over it again, how her brother told them about the Quit India movement, and about her party. But she doesn't go into the bit about speaking Hindi at home.

Naniji continues, "So, in the evening, one by one, friends came, but no one from Tilak's family. I remember how my mother kept looking out the dining-room window, over to Tilak's house. I didn't care, I just wanted my presents, and I wore my new clothes, and a jasmine garland in my hair."

I wipe away the onion tears with the back of my hand.

"Tea, Mummyji?" asks Mom.

"I'd love some."

I sigh and roll my eyes.

Naniji says placatingly, "I think we can sit for a while, no? I'll put the *bhaji* together afterwards. It'll only take a few minutes." She chuckles suddenly. "My goodness, you've cut that fine."

I've chopped the onion so hard, it's a soggy mess. Naniji looks into my eyes and smiles, like there's something just between the two of us.

As soon as she sits down and starts to sip her tea, I say, "*Now* will you please continue, Naniji?"

Naniji lowers her mug. "So then, at my party, everyone was finally there, and my mother brought in the cake, a nice chocolate cake with chocolate icing. God knows how she made it—there was severe rationing, she must have hoarded for ages to get the sugar and cocoa. We children were all sitting on the floor, on a *chuddar*—you know, a bedspread. And just as everyone finished singing 'Happy Birthday,' before I could even blow out the candles, we heard the noise next door—shouts. We all ran to the window."

Nina leans forward. Maya's eyes are riveted on Naniji.

"And there was a troop of British officers, taking away Tilak's father, and others were swarming into his house. There was such a shocked silence. I remember my mother, her hands pressed to her mouth, saying, *I hope Sarojini is all right.* That was Tilak's mother—your great-grandmother. Then, suddenly, our doorbell rang. And when the servant opened the door, in marched two British officers, followed by a troop of policemen."

Naniji blinks rapidly.

I grip the edge of the table.

"The first officer, he said he was looking for Arjun. My brother," she explains to Nina. "Arjun stepped forward, and the officer told him he was under arrest."

Mom's listening intently, caught up. It must be the first time she's heard this story, too.

"And Arjun said, *What am I charged with?*" Naniji sighs and shakes her head. "He was my big brother, seventeen, so brash. He was not supposed to be scared of anything. But his Adam's apple, it was bobbing up and down. I couldn't take my eyes off it. I knew he was frightened, and there was a sinking feeling inside me, like I was drowning."

She looks straight at me, like she's forgotten the others. "I'll never forget the look in that officer's eyes, Tara. Blue eyes, chips of ice, so full of contempt, like Arjun was a dog. No, not even a dog—just dirt."

My stomach feels sick and shaky.

Naniji continues. "He said something about seditious material and searching the house for Congress Party pamphlets—that was the main party fighting for freedom. Then my mother spoke up. She was so afraid, but angry, too. *There's no seditious material here. Can't you see there's a child's birthday party going on?*"

My hands are clenched in my lap. I'm frozen, caught in her past.

"And he looked down at my mother and snapped, *You natives! You think you can create all kinds of mischief and then hide behind a party.* And he lifted his stick and smashed it down on my cake."

Nina gasps. Mom bites her lip and holds Maya closer, rubbing her back.

"Then it was all confusion. The cake spattered brown blotches on my mother, my friends, Arjun, on my new yellow *salwar khameez*, everywhere. And the candles scattered and one or two burnt into the bed cloth and some of my friends screamed, and Mummyji, she stamped out the fire with her bare foot. And Arjun . . ." Naniji's voice falters. "Arjun moved forward, to stop him, and the officer, he brought the stick across his face. Then I don't know what happened, but Arjun's cheek was cut open, bleeding,

bleeding, all over his white clothes. Blood and cake were everywhere; he was being arrested, and one of his friends, too, who just happened to be there, and his friend was begging and pleading, saying how he wasn't even a Congress Party member, but it made no difference. And my aunts, my father's sisters, were crying, and the officers and police were tearing through things, searching, all over the house, and I could hear their boots thudding and Kunti, our cook, wailing, and I was so shocked that they went into the prayer room, the *prayer room*, and turned everything upside down."

My throat feels swollen.

"Of course they found nothing. Arjun and Papaji had been careful not to keep any incriminating material in the house. But they arrested Arjun anyway. And me, I was just standing there, frozen, I couldn't even cry, and Mumtaz, my best friend, was clinging to me, sobbing, sobbing. And, finally, they took Arjun and his friend, Arjun holding his cheek with his handkerchief, soaked red, and as they were going out the door, my mother"—Naniji draws in a long, shuddering breath—"my mother, who was normally so meek and mild, so careful not to get openly involved, she lifted her fist and she shouted, oh, she screamed, *Karengae ya marengae, we will do or die!*" Naniji's whole body is shaking.

For a long moment no one says anything.

I blink away the moisture in my eyes. "What happened?"

"They arrested her, too."

"Pigs!" says Nina fiercely.

Mom's face is pale as she rocks Maya.

Naniji continues, "And as they started to take her out, suddenly, I was able to move, and I leaped forward and I screamed, *Karengae ya marengae*, and Mumtaz, she was still crying, but she grabbed me and slapped both her hands on my mouth."

I can't breathe.

"The officer who'd hit Arjun, he turned around, eyes like fire, and he raised his *lathi*, and my mother screamed *no*, and the other officer tugged his arm and said, *She's just a child*. And the officer looked at me with so much hate, so much hate, but he let the other man pull him out. And I wrenched away from Mumtaz and ran to the door. She grabbed my hair to stop me, but just my jasmine garland tore off in her hands, and I reached the door and screamed, *Quit India, Quit India*, over and over, until the trucks disappeared."

Naniji wipes her face.

Slowly, Mom reaches out and grips her hand.

Naniji squeezes it, then blows her nose.

I sniff deeply. My voice is shaky. "How long? How long was your mother in jail? And your brother?"

"Oh, they let her go after a few days, unlike many of the others." Naniji looks scornful. "That's because the jails were overflowing with people. There were thousands arrested. You've no idea. So many had nothing to do with the freedom movement. Arjun, he was locked up for four months, then let go. But as soon as he came out he demonstrated and was rearrested. And Tilak. He joined a demonstration—you know, to protest the arrests—so they locked him away for three years." Naniji's face is grim. "But from that day, I knew the British did not have moral authority. I knew their superiority was a lie. I left the English school. I told Papaji I would *not* go. And I started to speak only Hindi at home."

There's a long silence. Then Mom abruptly lifts the mug to her mouth. Naniji glances at her, and her eyes come back to the present.

I wish they could just let go of all that—it's always there, a shadow.

"So that's when you got involved?" I ask quietly.

Naniji nods. "I told Papaji that I wanted to do my share, be actively involved."

"Did he let you?"

"Not at first. My mother talked him into it." Naniji smiles. "She was a strong woman, and she did her bit."

"Way to go, Naniji," says Nina.

Mom nods vehemently. "Good for her. Good for you."

Naniji flushes, her eyes bright.

"What did you do?" I ask.

"Oh, at first, I wanted to court arrest, but my mother convinced me that people were needed to help spread the real news about what was going on, the police violence. And she was worried, too, me being a girl, about me going to jail—terrible things happened, there were so many stories, you have no idea what horrors. I won't go into that. But I found out about the repression going on across the country, all that the British did. None of the newspapers were allowed to report it, not one. But we did." Her eyes are hard. "I helped to spread news from house to house, sometimes through word of mouth, sometimes by taking around the underground newspapers. And my father, he was so angry that they'd arrested my mother, he used his big black doctor's bag to carry news of our leaders from one house to another, right under the noses of the British. And my middle brother, Ramesh, he, too, became involved. That's when I took up spinning *khadi*."

"Spinning what?" asks Nina.

"Cotton," I say quickly. "Isn't that right, Naniji?"

Naniji nods. She glances at Mom again and licks her lips. "It changed my life, being part of it all—you can't imagine. The first time I attended a secret meeting, I just sat at the edge of the room, listening. I was the youngest, you know. But for the first time I felt like I was able to see clearly, think clearly. I had a sense of *belonging*. It was like coming out of the fog into sunshine, to be with people all part of a common purpose, a righteous purpose. It was so exciting. The first time I put up a poster saying *Quit India*—it was illegal, you know—I thought about that officer who arrested Arjun, and when I hammered in the nails it was his eyes I remembered."

"Yes!" I say.

Mom is nodding. And for that moment, we're united; we're all in the circle, hammering the poster with her *Quit India*.

Then the front door clicks open. Dad.

Maya runs to him and he picks her up and swings her around. "Me-Oh-Mayo!"

Naniji jumps up and hugs Dad. "My goodness," she says. "Look at the time." She rushes to the stove and turns on the burners. "I was telling Tara about the old days and I lost track. I'll get the dinner ready. Girls, we'll be eating soon." She stops abruptly, turns to Mom. "Of course, if it's all right with you, Rohini."

Mom's eyebrows flick upwards and her lips disappear. "Of course. Hello, Raj. How was your day?"

Dad's eyes dart from Naniji to Mom. "Er, fine, fine. Yours?"

"Fine." Mom smiles. "But I'm afraid I had to spend extra time at the shelter."

"Ahh, right, right." Dad's blinking too rapidly. "Smells good, Mummyji."

"Yes, *very* good," intones Mom.

But it's gone, that solidness, shattered. It's all awkward corners and angles. Artificial again. And I want . . . I want to pull it together.

"Hey, you missed something, Dad. Naniji was telling us about how she got started in the Independence struggle, about her fourteenth birthday and how her mother got arrested."

Naniji glances gratefully at me as she chops some green coriander leaves.

Dad seizes it eagerly. "Ah. Did she tell you about her shouting *Quit India* at the British officer?"

I snap around to look at Dad. "You knew about it?"

"Of course I knew; she's my mother."

"How come you never told us?"

"Yeah, Dad," says Nina.

Naniji's face is startled. Dad pushes what's left of his hair off his forehead. "Well, I did tell you about the arrests on Mummyji's fourteenth birthday, remember?"

"Just vaguely. All you told us was that members of her family were arrested—nothing about it being the middle of her party, or—"

"Yeah, Dad," says Nina. "The way you told us, it was so feeble."

Naniji gasps suddenly and lifts her finger to her mouth.

"Are you all right?" cries Dad.

"Yes, yes, just a little cut. The knife slipped."

"Let me see," says Dad.

"Wash it out under the tap," says Mom.

And they're fussing and fumbling, Naniji protesting that it's just a little cut, really it is, Dad overreacting, Mom stiffly solicitous, and Nina and Maya just watching.

In the end, I go for a Band-Aid.

CHAPTER
19

I don't pay much attention to the conversation over dinner. It drips and starts anyway, like before, even though it's less strained. Nina says something about trying civil disobedience in school, with one of the teachers, and Dad laughs while Mom pontificates about how there has to be a real cause. I just let it swirl around me.

I'm thinking about the assignment. How can I even start to write up something like that?

My eyes meet Naniji's.

We had this exercise one time in a creative-writing class, writing a fairy tale in the first person. Like it's happening to you. Maybe that's how I have to try this. Maybe it's the only way.

"You're awfully quiet, Tara," says Dad.

"I was just, you know, thinking about what Naniji told me earlier, and how to write it."

Mom says smoothly, "It's a powerful story, but I'm sure

you'll do it justice, Tara. If you need any help, well, I can give you some tips from my writing class."

That's all I need! But Mom looks so earnest, I just smile noncommittally.

After dinner, I rush up to my room and take out some lined paper. It's not due till Thursday, but I want to get it down now, while it's fresh. I start to write, feverishly. First person.

My heart pounds when I get to the officer bringing his stick down on the cake, and then I don't know how to spell *Karengae ya marengae*, but I manage anyway, and I scream in my head, *Quit India, Quit India*, scream with Naniji as I write it, and I can't help it, the tears stream down my face.

When I'm done I bury my face in my arms.

Holy shit.

My family. My history.

My family history.

I didn't expect it to be like this, I didn't. I wipe my face and blow my nose.

Then it hits me.

My class. They're mostly white. Some of them, a lot of them, their families must have originally come from Britain.

Maybe some of their ancestors were even part of the whole thing in India, the officer with the blue eyes smashing his stick. How . . . how will they take it when they hear it?

And how can I possibly read it, with all those white kids listening, and me feeling, I don't know, suddenly so, so—different? So brown.

I drop my head in my hands. This is crazy, it's totally crazy. It's not supposed to be like that here, is it?

Blue eyes.

I go icy cold.

Jeff's grandfather. He'd been everywhere, Jeff said, with the British army. *Even spent a few years in India.* He's a Brit—one of them—smashing her cake. Was he in India then?

For a long while I just sit there, arms limp in my lap, staring out the window.

This is the world I live in.

But how do I fit?

I'm not one of the true natives, the First Nations, and not one of the whites who marauded the globe colonizing, who tell the history of Canada from when they arrived. I'm too dark for the Samanthas and the rednecks, but not dark enough for Tolly, or Indian enough for Naniji, too Canadian, too western. Always *too something.* Never just right.

Except I was born here, this is my home, too; it's the only world I know. But how does it fit here—*do or die, Quit India*, even Naniji's face, as she told us what happened?

No. I can't read it, I can't. It'll make me so . . . conspicuous. Even if the others don't get mad, they'll think I'm—*Indian*; it'll just be falling in with Tolly's labels, letting them push me out further.

I look down at the pages in front of me.

Black and white. I've written it.

She lived through it.

In a way, I have to read it.

But Jeff—how will he take it? He's close to his grandfather, thinks he's great. . . .

I give myself a hard shake.

It'll be all right—Jeff and the others, they're not respon-

138

sible for what their ancestors did. It's not supposed to be about sides, is it? Not here.

Except, inside me, something's changed. There's something sharp that wasn't there before. It's a bit like after Samantha. No one understood then. No one can now.

I wrap my arms around myself. Erin's my best friend. She'll understand—won't she?

I pick up my violin and try to play, to reach that place of release, but somehow I can't get the notes right, and the violin wails with pain. It's early, only nine-forty-five, but I'm exhausted. I manage to change into my PJs and stumble into bed.

Just before I wake, I have a dream. I can't remember what's happened, but suddenly my whole class is there. Erin's beside me and Jeff, too, and we're all, even me, laughing and laughing. I can feel my belly shaking with deep, loosening laughter, and I feel weak and wonderful. I don't know what we're laughing at, but we're together, one, the whole group . . . in the middle of it the alarm goes. As I wake up, I'm still warm with laughter.

I sit up in bed, grinning.

Last night comes flooding back. My smile fades. How could I have laughed like that after last night?

Jeff. Blue eyes—no. I won't think about it. I get up and shower before Nina hogs the bathroom, then run down to breakfast.

It's just Naniji and me, and Mom and Maya. I eat in silence.

Mom looks at me penetratingly. "So how did you get on with your assignment?"

I swallow. "Fine. I finished it."

Naniji's face lights up—her smile is so much like Maya's. "May I see it, Tara, what you wrote?"

"Yes, I'd love to see it, too," says Mom quickly.

"Sure, maybe when I've tidied it up."

I finish my cereal and put my bowl in the sink. Mom comes up behind me and gives me a long hug.

I lean into her and kiss her cheek. I can feel how her body is tense, and I know it has to do with Naniji being here, and unfinished business, but it's not my problem. I have my own stuff to sort out.

Erin's early for once. I grab my bag and we set out.

It's a gorgeous sunny day, the kind only the fall brings, with vivid blue sky. It's at that perfect stage where the ground is radiant with fallen leaves, but there are still enough on the branches—red, yellow, orange—to make a glowing canopy. Not the kind of day to bring up . . . stuff.

"Hey." Erin digs me with her elbow. "What's up?"

"Nothing, just, you know, looking at the leaves and . . ."

"Yeah?" Her eyes narrow. "Jeff? Did you call him yesterday?"

I shake my head. Talking to him, everything from before, it seems so trivial, somehow.

Erin frowns. "Then what? Oh. Your grandmother, right? What happened?" Her eyes are alert.

My heart starts to hammer. I don't want to talk about it, and yet maybe this is my chance. I mean, if Erin doesn't get it, if she looks at me weird, I can write up something else for class. . . .

It's hard to bring that old story, the way Naniji told it, to this clear sunny day. It's like a rock, a boulder on top of a mountain. Slowly, I start to push it out, and then it picks up speed. Erin listens. She's my best friend, there's not a trace of racism in her. I watch for signs of the shutter coming down, but it doesn't. Her face is open, horrified, and then I'm not holding back anymore, and Naniji's story comes crashing out.

We stop at the park corner near the school as I finish telling her. Somehow, it makes it more real, saying it out loud, but also more distant, and I can't quite explain it, but by the time I'm done, I'm here in the present again, not lost back there.

"Oh my God!" says Erin.

I nod.

Erin shakes her head. "I mean, it's—*awful*. I sure as heck didn't know things like that happened." She looks at me sharply. "What did you feel like when she told you? I mean, what do you feel about her?"

I shrug. "I'm sort of okay with her. I mean, I still don't want her, you know, to change my life around or anything, but . . ." I pause. Should I try and explain that other thing? About feeling different, and wondering about the class, about Jeff and his grandfather?

Just as I open my mouth, we hear the bell ring.

"Oh jeez! Come on." Erin starts running towards school.

I manage to overtake her, and she comes puffing behind me.

"No fair," she pants. "You've got longer legs."

I laugh. "Barely."

Then we're in the school, and there are kids everywhere, noisy, laughing, and it's like it's always been, only it isn't quite. I'm not sure just what has changed, but something has.

In the hallway, I see Lesley, whose locker is two down from mine. She has blond hair. It's pretty. I've never really thought much about it, but Samantha, she had brownish-blond hair. What color was that officer's? Blond and blue go together sometimes, only Jeff's hair is dark, but that's irrelevant. It's just, Lesley's in my history class, too, and . . . what's she really *like*?

I shake myself. Leela's just started to go out with Phil, even though her parents and grandmother don't know about it, and he's white and she isn't, and it's no big deal. And Trev's going out with Jennifer—things here aren't the way they are in inner-city schools, with all that unrest and racial violence. We all mix together, we always have.

Except for the kids who've just come here. I notice Fatima and Ifran, together as usual, with the other Somali kids. And the Vietnamese kids, they hang out together. It's language, it must be.

But what if it isn't? Do they hang out together because they want to, or because we've pushed them out? I never bother talking to them much. Is it because they dress differently, because they don't look like us?

I flush. Who's us? And if I read Naniji's story, will it make me one of them, not us?

Then I see Jeff.

He pauses as he goes by.

"Tara . . ." he starts.

Blue eyes. Stick smashing down.

"Hi," he says lamely.

Tomorrow. I'm reading it tomorrow.

I can't meet his eyes. I manage an abrupt "Hi."

Jeff flushes, then goes slowly down the corridor. I turn back to my locker, my heart hammering painfully.

All through English, I have a tough time concentrating. I sit up front, and I know Jeff's sitting at the back. He's well out of my peripheral vision. Jessie's sitting next to him. *Stop it, Tara.* He never really liked me, and even if he did, once he hears what I'm reading tomorrow, he'll hate me. I force myself to listen to Ms. Gelder.

When the class is over, I gather my books casually and turn around. Jeff's already out of the room. I can't make out if Jessie's with him. Not that it matters.

Erin and I hang out at lunchtime with all the others, and I try not to look around the cafeteria for Jeff. But I can't help noticing again how it's mostly white faces, and I hate it, this being all cut up, strangled by lines.

"Tara." Erin shakes my arm. "What's with you?"

I force a smile. I've never bothered with the white–not-white thing before, it's totally nuts. I get caught up in the conversation going on at the table, but throughout the day, at odd times, it comes flashing back.

CHAPTER
20

I have a hard time falling asleep, and when I get up the next morning, I have a dull, heavy ache in my head. Thursday. I start to put my history folder in my bag, then stop. I could forget it at home. Tolly will be miffed, he might even take off marks, but . . .

I shove in my folder angrily. It's going to be fine.

In the kitchen, Mom's all concerned because I hardly eat any breakfast. She touches my forehead briefly. I could play sick so easily. But then I see Naniji's face, how she smiles at me, and I just can't.

It's a crappy day at school. I can't concentrate on math and I haven't a clue what the lesson is about—I'm going to have to call Nadia later to find out.

During English, Nadia and I sit together, and I do my best to look attentive so Gelder won't pounce on me again, but my mind keeps wandering and that cloudy feeling in my head gets worse. Maybe I am coming down with something. Jeff's sitting near the back, but I don't bother to look his way at all.

At lunchtime, I take a few bites of my sandwich and give the rest to Kim. Lesley and her crowd are right in my line of vision, Lesley with her blond hair and ditzy smile. She and her group, all white. I swallow hard. Fatima and Ifran are going by and I say hi brightly. They look surprised but say hi back.

Someone pokes me, and I try to concentrate on what we're talking about—some concert coming up.

History isn't till the last period today. Nadia and I get there early and sit near the back. Nadia's still going on about the concert, how she just has to go, and needing only another thirty-two dollars, and the chores she's doing to get it. I listen like I'm totally absorbed in her, but I'm hoping wildly that somehow Jeff won't show—a dentist appointment, anything—even though he was here this morning.

Jeff comes in and sits at the opposite end of the room from me. If I turn my head slightly, I see him. I should've sat up front again, and, boy, does Nadia ever go on and on about this dumb group.

Then Tolly's rapping on the desk. He looks even scruffier than usual, with his tight jeans and his wispy, frizzy hair dropping dandruff on his shoulders. Why the heck does he have to wear pointy shoes?

"All right, people, let's get this show on the road." He checks his list. "Guy, Jennifer, Rebecca, and Tara, you're on today. How did you get along?"

Guy, of course, sits up straight and says, *Great, just great.* Nadia nudges me.

Tolly eyes Jennifer, Rebecca, and me. Jennifer flushes. She hates reading out loud because she's so shy.

I slide my assignment into my folder. I'm not saying a word. I'm going last. Maybe there won't be time for me today.

"And how about you, Ms. Mehta? You're awfully quiet. Did you finish?"

I cover the folder with my hand and nod convulsively.

Tolly looks at me from under his shaggy eyebrows, frowns, then turns away.

"And the rest of you? People due tomorrow?"

Pete says something about talking to his grandfather about World War II.

Tolly nods up and down, up and down, in that way he has. "Good, good, good, good."

My fingers tighten around my pencil. World War II. That's when all that stuff happened to Naniji. What is Jeff writing about? What his grandfather did in India? *Went out and whacked a few natives on the head—jolly good sport . . .* ? Okay, so that's unfair, but . . .

Tolly clears his throat. "All right, people." He does a mini–drum roll on the desk with his fingers. "Who's first?"

I look carefully down, my heart beating unpleasantly.

"Guy Bériault," says Tolly.

For the first time, I'm glad Guy's such a little brown-nose.

Guy starts. I have a hard time taking it in. I have a vague idea it's something to do with his great-great-grandparents coming to Quebec, clearing the land, tapping the trees for maple syrup, getting through the winter. I don't really know what it's got to do with the assignment. It's not set against any moment in history, he's just giving us their entire frigging life stories—in excruciating detail.

Nadia sighs and rolls her eyes. I watch the others' faces, and mostly they're resigned, but I'm glad he has pages and pages. There won't be time for me today. I just have to rewrite my piece, do something different. I mean, Guy's, it's all so safe and—nice.

There's silence when he finishes.

Tolly clears his throat. "Well, people, comments."

No one says anything. Guy flushes.

Then Rebecca puts up her hand and says, "Um, it was, um, interesting."

She's so inarticulate. And maybe thinking about the fact that she might be next.

Tolly tries to get us talking about Guy's presentation, and a few more people say something polite, but, mostly, everyone's bored.

Finally, Tolly decides to move on. "Rebecca Fowler."

Rebecca clears her throat and starts to read. It's about her mother being in school in the U.S. when JFK was assassinated. I fade in and out. Rebecca's nice and everything, but she's way romantic, and I don't think anyone buys how her mother had this dreadful premonition. It should be emotional, but somehow it just doesn't feel real, the *searing, heart-wrenching, grieving nation*.

I shift uneasily. I can't possibly read mine, I'll look like a real idiot. I'm not like Mom with her in-your-face attitudes.

Rebecca finishes fast, way too fast. Again, there's the polite, bored silence, with Tolly trying to get reactions. I can hardly hear for the buzzing in my ears. Jennifer Resnick. She has to go next, she just has to.

Tolly says, "All right, now, let's see . . . ?" He looks at Jennifer.

Yes. Please. Pick her, pick her. I stare at his feet. Rule number one, never make eye contact with the teacher. Someone should tell him no one wears pointy-toed shoes anymore.

Tolly says, "Since we're proceeding alphabetically, I believe you're next, Ms. Mehta."

I try to think of something, anything, to get out of it.

"You have finished, haven't you?"

I nod. "Yeah, but . . . I . . . I don't really like reading out loud, and there're some changes . . ."

Tolly raises his shaggy eyebrows. "Hey, sorry, kiddo, it's a bit late for that, and you're going to have to read it aloud sometime."

Someone—Mike, I think—groans.

I lick my lips and look at the sea of faces. Mostly white, except for Trev in the corner, and a few others. I won't look at Jeff.

My hands are icy cold. I take in a deep breath. For Naniji. For a long line of revolutionary women. *Karengae ya marengae.*

"Okay, as long as I don't have to stand."

"Please. Sit. Sit, by all means," says Tolly, bowing slightly.

He adopts his usual storklike posture, one leg up on the chair, and waits expectantly.

CHAPTER
21

I start to read. I hope I won't fall apart in the middle of it. My heart is hammering, my voice sounds breathless, strange. But after a while it steadies. My throat goes tight through the screaming *Quit India* part, but I manage to keep going.

Then I stop.

There is absolute silence.

I flush. Okay, so they're all really mad, or they hate it, or they're laughing; or maybe it's just crappily written and it stinks. Or they're simply bored.

Only, there's something different about the silence. I bite my lip and fumble with the papers. My hands shake. Good thing Jeff's out of my line of vision.

Then Tolly whispers, "Wow!"

I look up. Everyone's staring at me. The room is charged.

"Damn!" someone mumbles.

"Quite remarkable, Tara," says Tolly, softly.

Lesley lifts a furtive hand to her cheek. Is she crying?

The mist sort of clears from my eyes. The class is still hushed. Jessie's mouth is slightly open. Rebecca's face is white, with freckles standing out. She looks at me quickly, then down at her folder; she bites her lip. Guy is silent, for once. All the faces are shocked, dismayed. But *with* me, I think, not *at* me. Jeff . . . ? I won't turn around.

Then I catch Pete's eye, and I see it, that troubled look, the shutter coming down.

"Comments, discussion?" asks Tolly quietly.

I feel my face burn.

Someone, Nadia, I think, lets out a sigh. "I didn't know any of that. I mean, you never read about that in textbooks."

There's a subdued chorus of agreement.

Tolly leaps on it. "Exactly the purpose of this exercise. Exactly. Come on, people. Reactions, comments."

Lesley mumbles, "It was really, you know, like—powerful. Moving." She sniffs.

Trev says, "Yeah, I can identify with that, man. A lot of crap like that went on in Uganda, too."

Someone asks, "Did it really happen?"

I nod. "To my grandmother."

A murmur washes through the room.

I don't hear Jeff's voice.

But I see how Lynne is shifting uneasily, and as she catches my eye, she blinks rapidly and turns away. One time I overheard her making fun of Fatima's accent. Shutters. And I see it on Mel's face, too.

Ben says, "Well, it's awful and everything, but it was a

long time ago, so what's the . . ." His voice fades, and he shrugs slightly. *What's the big deal?*

Then Pete says, slowly, "Hey, don't get me wrong or anything, Tara, but, you know, the time you're talking about, well, my grandfather was in France, fighting in the trenches, and my grandmother, she was in London, and the bombs were falling and . . . I don't know. What happened to your grandmother really sucked big, but, but my family wasn't really part of it, and . . . and it was an awful time for Britain, too. . . ." He's turning redder and redder, and his eyes are troubled, defensive.

"Yeah, right on," says Mel. But it's different how he says it, like a *so there.*

I draw in a painful breath. Everyone likes Pete, and what happened to his grandparents was awful. If that's how Pete feels, what is Jeff . . . ?

I can't help it, my head turns. Jeff's pale, his face tight. His eyes are down, like he isn't even here.

Abruptly, he looks straight at me, his eyes leaping blue—puzzled, angry.

I swivel back to Tolly, my heart thumping. So that's how it is.

Tolly clears his throat. "Well, Tara's excellent presentation demonstrates superbly the need to examine history from alternate points of view."

He says it like he's a super-cool teacher for giving us this awesome assignment. Nadia makes a gagging motion.

Tolly continues. "Pete brings up a good point. What was happening in England at the time. And here, too. Canadian men, er, and women, at war." He grins. "I guess we plain old regular Canadians need to know the history of other places to get a real and balanced view."

Plain old regular.

As in white.

It jolts through me like lightning. I almost bought his idea of regular—*that's* why I was afraid to read Naniji's story. In case it made me different, not a regular Canadian. I almost bought it!

Suddenly, everything falls into place, diamond-sharp. I know where I fit. This is my home, and no one—*no one*—is pushing me out.

My heart races like it's going to burst, but I have to say it. "Mr. Toller, I *am* a regular Canadian."

"Pardon?" Tolly looks at me.

"I *am* a regular Canadian," I repeat.

There's a sudden silence, then a few voices. "Yeah, she is." "So am I."

Lynne's face is wary; Nadia, Ben, and a few others look surprised.

Tolly says quickly, "No, no, all I meant—"

I interrupt, "I know what you meant, sir, but maybe you need to expand *your* idea of a regular Canadian." Blood pounds in my face. I don't care if that's rude, but I'm not taking it back, not if I get detention, not even if everyone thinks I'm overreacting. I sit straight and stare directly at him.

Someone says, "Right on."

Trev says, "You go, girl."

And Lesley says loudly, "Yeah, it's all this grouping crap that makes trouble, all this defining."

There's a chorus of agreement, and I think I hear Jeff's voice, but I'm not sure, and I'm not looking again, I can't.

Tolly smiles awkwardly. He bobs his head up and down. "Of course. I stand corrected."

Okay, so he's a dork, I mean, those pointy shoes, but at least he heard what I said, he listened. I don't know if he quite gets it, but I can see he's trying. I manage a shaky smile and scan the class.

Most of the kids are nodding. But Lynne and Mel are still shuttered, and a few others are puzzled. They just don't get why it's a big deal; they probably think I'm a real freak, bringing it up.

My heart twists. All these faces, all these stories. There's such a chance to interweave and come together here. It could be so different.

For a split second I have the same feeling I had in the dream that night, all of us *together*. Then it's gone and I'm back in the class with old friends—but there's also Pete, who is troubled; Nadia, who's never thought about *regular Canadians* and who still doesn't get it; and Lynne, whose laughter is at, not with; and Mel; and Jeff. But mostly friends.

Doug says gruffly, "Yeah, Mr. Toller, we don't need stuff like that. We're a brave new world and—"

Lesley bursts out laughing. "Brave new world. Doug, have you even read the book? D'you know what it's about?"

Tolly says, "Now, wait a minute, I think what Doug meant was . . ."

Doug mutters, "Jeez, why's she freaking?"

Lesley rebuts, "Read the book, moron, and try to get the metaphor right."

Just then the bell goes.

I start to gather my things and turn around casually. Jeff glances my way, his face grim.

I turn to Nadia and flash on a huge smile. "So—about that concert, how much are the tickets?"

Nadia looks at me like I've got two heads. "I've only told you about three thousand times."

"So tell me again."

Jeff's standing at his desk as we walk past. My face is turned to Nadia like I'm totally absorbed by what she's saying.

As we walk towards our lockers, a few of the kids slap my back and say, "Amazing story, Tar," or "That was awesome."

No sign of Jeff. I swallow the bitter taste in my throat.

Erin's waiting by her locker. Just as I get there, I feel someone's arms go around me from behind.

Lesley.

"That must have been so . . . difficult, Tar, and, well . . . I just want to say thanks."

I smile, hug her back. She squeezes my hand and bounces along.

I open my locker slowly. All those things I thought about her, because of her blond hair. I bite my lip. It's not just about other people's lines. It's also about me not adding to it.

Erin says, "What was that about?"

I look at her. "Oh, my history assignment. I read it today."

"Yeah? How'd it go?"

I put my books in my bag and say, "Pretty well. I think. But it was, well . . ."

Erin's face is puzzled. "Lesley sounded like it went over big."

As we walk home, I tell her. It's such a relief to let it out—how I felt different, how I wondered about the reaction I'd get. I hesitate, then tell her about Jeff's grandfather. Erin's eyes widen. Only it's not about Jeff, so I hurry on, and I know I'm not very coherent, but she listens intently. She nods, at times she looks puzzled, but still she listens, and it's one of the things I love so much about her.

When I get to the bit about Tolly and *regular Canadians*, she gasps, "What? Shit! What did you say?"

I tell her.

"Way to go, Tar! And what did the other kids say?"

I tuck my hair behind my ear. "I don't know, it's like most of them got it, but a lot didn't. I mean, Nadia, she had this puzzled look. It wasn't like Lynne—sort of distant and *Who cares?*—but I know she didn't understand. Nadia had this *Why does this matter so much?* kind of expression."

Erin shakes her head. "Nadia's not the brightest bulb."

"But she wasn't the only one."

Erin puts her arm around me. "That's really crappy." She looks at me sharply. "What about Jeff?"

I shrug. "I don't know. But right after I finished reading, he . . . he looked mad."

Erin's arm tightens. "You okay?"

"Yeah." I grin at the concern in her face. "Hey, what d'you expect—Jeff's close to his grandfather and probably thinks it's some sort of criticism of him."

Erin hesitates then says, "You sure it's that?"

"Come on, what else could it be?"

"I don't know. I'm surprised at Jeff. I mean, it's not like him to—"

"Drop it, Erin, I don't want to talk about him. If he can't take it, too bad. What matters is that I read it."

Erin nods vehemently. "Right on."

I hold on to that satisfaction; I wrap it around me like a flag.

CHAPTER
22

As we turn the corner onto my street, I pick up speed. I can't wait to tell Naniji. I strain to see our driveway. Is Mom home? She'll be pretty thrilled, too, especially that I stood up to Tolly. As we get closer, I make out Mom's and Dad's cars. Well, whaddya know.

I wave goodbye to Erin and shout, as I open the door, "Hi, I'm home."

They're all in the kitchen—Dad at the stove; Mom, Naniji, Nina, and Maya at the table. Oh yeah, Dad's night to cook. Smells like his spaghetti sauce. I'm surprised Naniji let him—Mom probably insisted, to make the point!

Naniji beams at me as she sips her tea. "Tara. How was your day?"

"Great."

Mom tilts her head. "What's up, pet?"

I drop my bag on the floor and announce, "I did my

history assignment. You know, the stuff Naniji told us, I read it today."

"Oh, and I haven't seen it yet," cries Mom.

Dad turns around, wiping his hands.

Naniji gets straight to the point, her eyes alert. "And what was the reaction?"

There's a sudden silence.

I grin. That's so Naniji.

"Well, there were some people who were defensive about it. . . ." I tell them about Pete, and even Lynne and Mel and the shutter. I tell them how most of them listened, how everyone was silent, because it was all too much. I tell them about Lesley, but not everything, not what I'd thought about her. I don't say a word about Jeff.

Naniji nods, grimly pleased. "Thank you, Tara."

"Good for you," says Mom quietly.

Dad thumps my back. "Yes, it's something people need to know about."

I laugh. "Yeah, that's what Tolly said. And then, guess what? He says something about how regular Canadians need to know about this kind of—"

"What?" squeaks Nina.

Mom's eyebrows fly upwards. "Well! It seems there's no end to this poor man's confusion. Tara, dear, I really think I need to have a gentle little word—"

I burst out laughing. "No, Mom, I took care of it."

"Did you tell him to drop dead?" asks Nina eagerly.

Mom frowns at Nina, then turns to me.

"No, but I said I *am* a regular Canadian, and, you know, a lot of kids joined in. I mean, a few of them didn't get it, why it mattered, but mostly there was a chorus of support, and I got the point across. I spoke out, I did it. All by myself."

"*Well done*, Tara," says Mom, beaming. "Well done, *indeed!*"

Oh God, she's looking at me like I'm a carbon copy of her.

"Regular," says Maya importantly. "I'm regular Canadian, too."

The knot at the back of my neck loosens. It's such a relief to be home, where they understand. I glance at Naniji; at Dad, who's smiling and nodding; then, abruptly, back at Naniji. Her face is grave and shuttered.

What? Now what?

"Regular Canadian," murmurs Maya.

Naniji's eyes flick upwards.

Is *that* it?

Naniji catches me staring and tries to smile. She's stiff, but it's not like before, with the criticism and disapproval, and the hostility. Her eyes—they're hurt.

I'm floored. I mean, we've connected. We can't go back to that old antagonism; it's not how I feel about her. But I can't take back what I said. I'm proud of what she did, proud it's my heritage, but this is my life, and I had to say what I did to Tolly. I had to—it's part of who I am, how I fit here.

Mom's noticed, too. She's smiling awkwardly.

Dad clears his throat and says a shade too heartily, "Well, are we ready to eat soon?"

Naniji makes herself smile. "My goodness, my poor son cooking for his mother."

Mom flushes but refrains from a retort. Nina winks at me.

It's a bit easier when we sit down to eat half an hour later, but only slightly. I'm still elated, but also jittery about Naniji, and starting to get mad. I read it, didn't I? What more does she want? It's bad enough that some of the class didn't get it; I don't need that here as well.

Nina's rattling on about this kid in her class who got kicked out for swearing at the teacher, and Mom jumps in with her opinion of what's really troubling him.

Naniji's quiet, lost in thought.

I offer an olive branch. "Say, Naniji. Maybe sometime you can tell me all about the stuff you did with the underground newspapers, huh? And I can write it down, too, sort of for family history."

Naniji gathers herself together. "Yes, Tara, of course, if you want." But the fire's gone out of her. She turns to Dad. "Raj, over the next few days we should call the airline and book my return flight."

I freeze.

Dad says, "Mummyji, you can't go this soon. . . ."

Mom says, "No, of course you should stay longer. . . ." She's not entirely convincing.

My heart squeezes painfully. Is she going because of what *I* said? I blurt, "Naniji, don't go already, we . . . ."

Naniji smiles. "Thank you all. Very much. No, I don't mean I have to go at once, just within a couple of weeks. But we have to arrange it."

"Oh," says Mom. I see how her shoulders ease as the unknown duration of the visit is lifted.

"But even then," says Dad, "what's the hurry?"

160

"Well, I may not work, but I do have volunteer boards I sit on, and they require attention."

"Yeah, but you have to stay for Halloween," I say quickly. "You don't have Halloween in India, do you?"

Naniji shakes her head.

Nina says, "You have to come with us for our annual pumpkin hunt. You'll love it, Naniji."

Naniji looks puzzled. "Pumpkin hunt?"

Nina says, "Yeah, we go to the market to buy the biggest pumpkins for Halloween, and scoop them out and carve faces, you know, and put candles inside. Say, Mom, I've got to get a new mask this year. Tiff and I, and the gang, are going as bums and . . ."

"It's on October 31," says Dad to Naniji. "Children go out dressed up in costumes, and people give them candy."

"I *love* Halloween," sighs Maya.

"It sounds like fun," says Naniji. Then, quietly, warily, "And this year Divali is the first week of November."

"Yeah?" says Nina.

Naniji asks casually, "Do the girls know about Divali?"

Oh, great!

Mom says hastily, "They know a little, but, you know, what with school, and all their other activities . . ."

"Oh yeah," chips in Nina. "Fireworks and stuff. We did that one year, Mom and Dad took us to the temple or something."

"It was fun," I say, overeagerly. Actually, we were kind of bored. We hardly knew anybody, and all they let us kids have were those feeble little sparklers. On the way home Dad had gone on apologetically about how great Divali,

the festival of lights, is in India, with fireworks everywhere. Then Nina threw up in the car because she'd
gorged on too many Indian sweets, and somehow no one
really wanted to go through it again.

Dad shifts uneasily. "Well, it's not the same here, not like
Delhi. . . ."

Naniji is smiling, but she's stiff, so stiff.

Nina grimaces at me.

My mouth tightens. Naniji's acting like a spoiled brat.
I'm not going to let her retreat. I ask firmly, "So—what
boards do you sit on in India, Naniji?"

Naniji gives herself a little shake and looks up. "Well,
one of them is to raise money for cataract operations. You
know, the eyes, to cure blindness. And the other is similar
to the work your mummyji does. It's to help women who
are abandoned by their husbands."

"Hey, cool," I say.

Mom smiles. "Yes, I'm sure it's enormously beneficial."

Something the two of them have in common. Who'd
have thought?

I seize it eagerly. "Yeah, it's really needed there, too, isn't
it? Mom's told us about how difficult it is for women in
India."

Naniji's smile freezes.

What now? She brought up the shelter.

Naniji says tightly, "Yes, there is need, of course there is,
but so is there here."

"Well, yeah," I falter.

Mom says, guardedly, "Of course."

Naniji's eyes glitter. "In many ways, it's better in India, compared to here. In fact, there are fewer single-parent families in India. The divorce rates just aren't as high."

I see the alarm in Dad's face as Mom lifts her head like a warhorse going to battle. I try frantically to think of something to say, anything, but I'm too late.

Mom's voice is creamily dangerous. "Yes, but is it because marriages necessarily work better, or is it because women have fewer choices?"

Naniji flushes bright red and says sharply, "We aren't as backwards as you think. There are laws giving equality to women, and changes are taking place."

Mom raises her eyebrows.

Dad interjects, "Mummyji, Rohini didn't mean—"

Naniji continues, "I'm perfectly aware of how the west considers everything Indian to be primitive, but I thought *you* at least would teach the girls in a more balanced way."

There's an ugly silence.

"What do they know about India? Do they know anything about the art, the spirituality? Mahatma Gandhi? No, they hardly even know about the Independence struggle. I can't imagine what your papaji would think."

My heart hammers. I blurt, "Dad has told us some of it. . . ."

Dad's face is pale. "Mummyji, that's not fair."

"Isn't it? You don't even speak Hindi; you've never brought the girls to India. How can the girls know anything about their heritage? All they know is Canadian, Canadian, Canadian."

Oh God, no.

Mom's face turns scarlet. "You've never been able to accept that, you've always—"

"No, I can't accept that." Naniji's voice is forceful. She looks at Mom, then at Dad. "I can't accept that you, your father's son, left your country when there is so much need. Yes, we have problems there, but at least I'm doing something about it. I stayed."

Dad flinches. Mom turns pale with anger. Nina's eyes are wide with shock, and Maya has stopped chewing and is staring.

Mom's words spill out in a torrent: "It always comes back to that, doesn't it? You've never been able to accept our decision. Or me."

Naniji's eyes flash. "And did you even try to fit into our family? Did you try to accommodate at all to our way of life, our values?"

"Mummyji, please," says Dad. "Don't start."

Maya is rocking back and forth.

Mom snaps, "Why is it that you always expect *women* to accommodate and change? Why can't you accept that it was also Raj's choice to live here?"

Naniji raises her eyebrows. "Was it really—"

"Stop it, both of you." It's Dad. "You're frightening the children."

For a moment everyone's frozen. Then Maya's eyes brim over and she starts to howl.

Mom reaches for Maya and holds her close. Dad pushes his chair back and goes to them.

My head spins. Nina's face is white and bewildered. I go over and hug her.

"Jeez," she whispers. "What the hell happened?"

Dad's arms come around us. I turn and hold him.

He's sweating and his underarm smells a bit, but I hold on anyway. He's my dad and I wish . . . I don't know. He should have told us more. He should stand up to Mom more, to Naniji even. But he's not perfect, and that smell of him, it's real, and this is how he is—only human. Flawed. Like me.

Nina buries her face in his shoulder and starts to cry, and he pats her back. I pull away and take in a few deep, shuddering breaths.

I look around.

Naniji's gone.

CHAPTER
23

I go into the hallway and stand at the top of the basement stairs. My hand shakes on the banister.

A wave of anger washes over me. It's a freaking pattern. Pushing people out. She did it then, to Mom, and now she's doing it to us. Not good enough for her, not Indian enough. She has her say and then she runs away to the nice, cozy room we all slaved to fix for her. End of discussion.

She's not getting away with it. Not this time. I've been pushed out enough. I won't let her do it, too.

I start downstairs, my rage mounting with each step.

Her door is shut. I knock, *bang bang bang*. I don't wait for an answer, I fling open the door.

She's sitting there, on the wicker rocker, her mouth all tight and judgmental, her hands clasped, clutching to her views.

I march in and stand in front of her. She has the same

look of self-righteous anger she had when she first came here, and, yes, she's formidable all right.

I don't even try to hide how mad I am. "You have no right!" I spit out the words. "You have no right to come marching into our lives and criticizing everything, because it's not your life. In case you haven't noticed, it's not 1942 anymore—"

Naniji's eyes flash fire. "How dare you—"

I drown her out. "What gives you the right to keep pushing us away? So you don't like that I'm a regular Canadian. Well, tough. I am. But I'm still . . ." I choke, but carry on. "I'm still your granddaughter, and why can't that be enough? I did it for *you* today, in school, I did it for you, but also for me. It's the same as you screaming *Quit India*, why can't you see that? I'm fighting for *my* place in the world, trying to get rid of that old colonial crap, and it's just as *revolutionary*"—I hurl that word at her—"as what *you* did, and, anyway, if it means so damn much to you, why"—I hate how the tears fill my eyes and spill over—"why the *hell* didn't you come visit before?"

She starts back, like I've slapped her.

Angrily, I wipe my face with the backs of my hands. I had no idea that was coming out; I didn't even know it was there.

She reaches for me.

I move back, but she pulls me towards her and holds me.

I don't know how long I cry against her shoulder. She rocks me, her face wet against mine, her hand smoothing large, unhurried circles on my back.

Then I pull away and look around for the tissues. She

takes one and passes the box to me. I grab a handful and stand up, turn away from her.

This isn't how I'd wanted to do it.

When I look at her again, she's sitting still, in that way she has, but she looks shattered. She tries to smile but doesn't make it. Her eyes are devastated. Defeated.

I can't bear it. I drop on my knees beside her and reach for her hand. I stroke it gently.

She grips mine hard. She hesitates, then says slowly, "My God." A long pause, then, "How you remind me . . . you remind me of how I was. . . ." She tries to smile. "So fierce, so independent. So certain."

I don't know what else to say. She should have come before, but there's nothing I can do about that now.

Except, maybe, let her in.

I say quickly, before I can change my mind, "I'm sorry about how I treated you when you first came here, Naniji, you know, about the violin. If you want, I'll play it for you, and I'm sorry about all that other stuff, I'm—"

She shakes her head and puts her hand on my mouth.

I say, "But I'm glad you came, really I am, you should have . . ." I stop.

She manages, "Better late than never, no?"

I nod and sit back on my heels.

"Naniji," I say softly, "please come back upstairs. You need to talk and, and . . ."

Naniji's face closes again.

"You can't just leave it. Mom and Dad, especially Dad, you know, they do care, and . . . and you can't . . . you can't keep shutting us out." I add desperately, "I promise I won't open my mouth this time."

Unexpectedly, Naniji chuckles. "Somehow, Tara, I doubt it."

My jaw drops.

"See?" She's giggling, and I am, too, and then we're chortling together.

Finally, we stop.

Naniji looks terribly tired. "All right. Let's go up." She sighs faintly. "All these old, old tensions. I know . . . I know some of it . . . Never mind. One of the things about getting older is you learn—this, too, will pass." She smooths her hair. "First, I must wash my face."

I swing my arms restlessly as she goes into the bathroom. *Okay, Tara, keep it cool, just take it easy.*

She's in there a long time, a long time.

At last she comes out.

"Come," she says simply.

I see how she's taking in a deep breath and how her eyes are apprehensive. *Do or die.* Another battle, but a different demon. Please, please, let it be all right.

We go up the stairs. It's funny, she's not arthritic or anything, but she is in her seventies, and she's slow coming up. I've never noticed it before.

But, then, I've never climbed these stairs with her before.

I match my pace to hers, and we go up together, step by step.

CHAPTER
24

They're all sitting around the kitchen table. It's still littered with plates and food.

Mom's eyes flicker anxiously to me.

Dad gets up. "Mummyji." He looks both anxious and defiant.

She's his mother. I see the love and pain in her face as she reaches up silently and holds him.

I glance at Mom. There's no Marmee. No self-righteousness. Her face is still and sad. My throat closes over.

Naniji pulls away and smiles. She looks embarrassed. Her eyes lock with Mom's.

"Rohini," she says.

Dad says quickly, softly, "Mummyji, I'm sorry if it hurts you, but this is our life now. We . . . we live here, this is our home and . . . and I'd like you to accept that." His mouth shakes unexpectedly. "I'd like you to accept my . . ."

Mom turns crimson.

Naniji goes to her. Mom gets up, and, awkwardly, Naniji puts her arms around her.

Maya's eyes are round, and Nina gapes.

Naniji moves back and looks at Mom steadily.

Please don't let it fall apart again.

"Tara . . ." Naniji takes a deep breath. "Tara said I should have come before."

Dad looks surprised.

Naniji continues, "And she's right. I . . ." She clears her throat. "I know this, it's difficult, but . . ."

Don't blow it now, please, Naniji.

Her eyes turn towards me, almost like she hears my thoughts, then back to Mom. She swallows. "Sometimes it's difficult to change, but, I . . . I am thankful for how happy Raj is with you. . . ."

Mom's eyes fill.

Naniji continues, "And the children, my grandchildren, they're . . ." Naniji pauses, then says, with her irrefutable air of authority, ". . . *wonderful.*"

Nina's eyebrows fly upwards in an uncanny imitation of Mom. I smile faintly and bite my lip.

"So, it seems, there's much to be . . . grateful for, and, well"—Naniji looks at Mom, then Dad—"I know perhaps when you got married I may not . . ."

Mom blinks hard and says thickly, "It's . . . it's all right, Mummyji. I should have tried more, too. I'm sorry."

I let out my breath.

Dad's arm comes around Mom, his face a mixture of strain and relief. "Thank you, Mummyji," he says quietly.

Then Mom's sniffing on his shoulder, trying to pull herself together, and Naniji's stroking Dad's back.

I turn to Nina and make a face, anything to stop this stupid lump in my throat. She grins at me, her eyes very bright. Maya is watching, but, thank God, she isn't crying.

Mom lifts her head from Dad's shoulder and blows her nose briskly. She turns to us and flashes her biggest, brightest Marmee smile.

"I'm sorry, girls, if any of this has been, well, unsettling for you. And especially, you know, for any raised voices. Aren't we, Raj?"

Dad mumbles, "Er, yes, we . . ."

Naniji's eyes are startled.

And it's so Mom, it's so ludicrous and blessedly familiar, that I have to choke down the crazy laughter that bubbles upwards.

Mom turns to Naniji and asks graciously, as though they'd *never* screeched at each other, "Tea, Mummyji?" She offers it as the ultimate healing gift.

I bite my lip. I have to get out of here before I blow it again. I slide towards the back door. Nina looks up. I wave and shut the door behind me. Alone in the darkness, I stand still and let myself grin.

Then, cautiously, I make my way into the backyard.

It's chilly out here, dark except for rectangles of light from the Lings' house, and from the Gauthiers', and the light streaming from our kitchen window.

I wrap my arms around myself and lie flat on top of the picnic table. It's good to be by myself in the chill, clear night—the *clean* night.

Exhaustion washes over me in waves.

This morning seems like years away—light-years.

Jeff. Was that really today? A ghost of pain curls inside me. But I can't make myself care right now.

I gaze at the stars. Billions. Trillions. Dots. Constellations are all in our heads, just a game of connect-the-dots. Up there, all they'd see is our whole solar system, reduced to a single dot. So simple. I feel on the brink of some essential understanding, but then it's gone.

"Tara?"

I sit up. It's Nina.

"Hey, move," she says.

I make room for her, and she puts her arm around me. I put mine around her. It's not that cold, but still.

"Jeez!" says Nina. Then, after a while, "What did you do to get her to come up?" Her voice is a mixture of incredulity and admiration.

I tell her about it.

Nina lets out her breath. "Holy shit," she says.

We sit quietly for a while. Then Nina nudges me and points at the kitchen window. Mom's filling Naniji's cup, and Dad's holding Maya, who's saying something. Maya scrambles onto Naniji's lap, and Mom turns around, her mouth moving; and Dad pushes the hair off his face, in that awkward way he has.

It's all been *so* awful; I don't know who starts, but we're giggling. It's just nerves and hysteria, but suddenly it's hilarious, seeing Dad waving his arms around, Mom talking animatedly, Naniji nodding, more restrainedly.

"I don't know what's so funny," gasps Nina between spurts of laughter.

"Curry rice, very, verrry nice," I sputter.

And we're both shrieking, doubled with laughter.

Gradually, the spasms of laughter stop, except for the odd chuckle bursting out.

Nina shivers. "Come on, let's go in."

So we go in together, arms still twined around each other.

Maybe sometime I'll tell her about Jeff.

CHAPTER
25

The house feels strange as I go down to breakfast the next morning. Quiet. Mom's humming softly as she stirs some frozen orange juice. She looks worn, but somehow way less tense than she has lately.

She kisses me. "Morning, sweetie." She strokes my cheek and looks into my eyes. "You okay?"

"Yeah. I'm okay."

From the basement comes the distant sound of a toilet flushing.

"Sounds like your naniji is up," says Mom. "I'd better put the kettle on." She smiles, but her eyes are wary.

It's such a huge relief to be out in the crisp air with Erin, away from all those old complications. Back into my safe, normal life.

"I've got a lot to tell you," I start.

She turns to me eagerly. "Jeff called."

"No."

She makes a face. "Sorry."

"Hey, it's no big deal."

A slight pause before Erin says, "Okay, so what is it?"

Her eyes widen as I get into it.

When I tell her how I sounded off to Naniji, she lets out a crack of laughter. "That's so you, Tara."

We arrive at school laughing.

But my chest tightens as we go through the front doors. Was it just yesterday—that whole thing in class?

I look at the faces as we head down the corridor, past the throngs of kids. It's like I'm noticing things, seeing more clearly now.

Faces caught up in their own little lives. Leela's laughing up at Phil. Is she ever going to tell her parents about him? Fatima and Ifran are together, as always, with their Somali friends.

The way I've felt the last few days, the way I felt after Samantha, is that how they feel? Only all the time? Is that why they hang out with other Somali kids?

Lynne's coming out of the gym with Ben, Mel, a few others.

I feel a flood of panic. I want to go back to not noticing.

Lynne's eyes flicker as she sees me. She mumbles something to Ben, and his eyes swivel in my direction. They laugh.

For a second it feels like I can't breathe. Erin hasn't noticed.

I swallow.

This is the world I live in.

There's Erin and Lesley, but also Lynne, who wants to live in her own familiar little world. She probably thinks there are way too many immigrants here, forgetting that we're all, except the First Nations people, immigrants. When she sees me, she probably sees color, not Tara—sees different. I guess Lynne wants to keep it easy.

Just like the crybaby inside me wants to keep it easy. Maybe it's what too many people want.

My heart twists. It's obviously what Jeff wants.

Only I didn't expect it of him. I feel a surge of anger that surprises me.

"Hi, Tar," Lesley slaps my back, gives me a wide grin, and rushes on.

I've never noticed before what a great smile she has. Silver linings.

English is the last period today.

I stride down the corridor. I want to get there early so I can sit well up front this time. It's less distracting with most of the kids behind you.

Nadia comes running up beside me and starts jabbering away.

Through the kids milling around, I see Jeff. He's standing outside the class like he's waiting for someone.

Probably Jessie.

He looks straight at me. Why can't Nadia shut up for once?

"Tara," he bursts out.

I almost walk past, then stop abruptly. It's my world. It's up to me how I make it.

Nadia continues on into the classroom, still talking. She hasn't noticed I'm not there.

"I want to talk to you, Jeff," I say quickly.

Jeff's face is a mixture of relief and alarm. "Good, I want to talk to you, too."

We move around the corner and into a small empty classroom.

"Jeff, you have to . . ."

At the same time, he starts, "Listen, Tara . . ."

We both stop.

My heart is hammering unpleasantly, but I make myself look at him calmly and say, "I'm going first."

He flushes and shrugs. "Go ahead."

"About yesterday."

"Yeah, I want to talk about that, too." His blue eyes are sharp.

My stomach feels sick. I was right, he was mad, he didn't get it. Suddenly, I'm furious.

"Well, before you get on your high horse, just listen for one damn minute. What I read yesterday, it's part of my family, and I don't exactly understand how, but it's part of claiming my place here. But that doesn't mean I'm jumping on some kind of ethnic bandwagon, or buying into that old conflict, and you've got *no* right to get pissed off about it."

He opens his mouth, but I say, "Just shut up and listen. I mean, did you even hear Tolly getting into the thing about *regular Canadians*? I had a big fight with my grandmother about it, because she can't accept it, but the same thing applies to you."

He says, "What?"

"Just because I read it doesn't mean I'm any less Canadian. And it's not about what your grandfather did or didn't do, not here. It isn't supposed to be our fight. It's great that you're close to him, but if you want to get all bent out of shape and make a big issue about it, then go right ahead and—"

"What the hell are you talking about?" Jeff's face is indignant.

"Yesterday, when you—"

He interrupts. "Tara, would you just shut up before you make a complete and total ass of yourself?"

My mouth falls open. I turn to leave, but he catches my arm.

"Oh no you don't." He enunciates every word. "You're not walking out on me after that little speech. Now, *what* are you talking about?"

I take in a deep breath. "Yesterday. You were so mad at my story—"

"No, I wasn't."

"Yes, you were, I saw your face."

He laughs scoffingly. "Yeah? For the whole millisecond you condescended to look my way? You know, I've had it with your princess act."

"Princess?"

"Yeah. You can't just pick me up and drop me—"

"I didn't. You're the one who—"

"Then why the hell have you been freezing me out since the weekend?"

"I haven't . . ." I stop. "Okay, so I'm sorry about last weekend, but I thought you were still mad, and this isn't about that, so don't try and twist it around. It's about . . ." My voice fades.

He's looking at me steadily, but there's anger in his eyes.

"Thanks a lot, Tara. It's great to know you have such a high opinion of me. Listen. I was upset yesterday because your story was so awful. And . . . and," he stammers, "because I . . . I thought maybe you were mad at me, about my grandfather, and I sort of got mad at you for . . ."

Relief and anger arc through me. "Nice to know you have such a high opinion of me," I snap.

"Well, I guess that makes us even."

For a moment we just eye each other and say nothing, but that queasy feeling in my stomach is subsiding.

Jeff says, awkwardly, "I wanted to tell you yesterday. What Pete said, not everyone feels like that. I mean, I don't." He flushes. "Don't get me wrong, I love my grandfather and everything, but—"

"I know," I say impatiently.

"But it's not about that, is it?" His eyes are pleading. "I mean, it can't be. Not here. Not now."

The gush of release is so delicious, I have to roll my eyes, and say sarcastically, "What the hell d'you think I've been trying to tell you?"

Slowly, Jeff's face breaks into a crooked grin. He shakes his head and mouths, "Princess."

I whack his shoulder, and he laughs.

Just then the bell goes.

"Come on." Jeff tugs me towards the door. Okay, so he's holding my hand way too long, but I grip his anyway, even though my hand is all sweaty, or maybe it's his.

We sit together at the very back of the class.

"So," whispers Jeff, "what're you doing this weekend?"

"Nothing much." I quirk an eyebrow at him. "What did you have in mind?"

He grins. "Want to show me around some more?"

"Sure. And afterwards, you can come home with me and practice your Scottish accent."

Ms. Gelder clears her throat and looks warningly at us.

I sit up, pretend to be absorbed in what she's saying.

After a while, Jeff passes me a note. I open it cautiously, on my lap. I choke. In Jeff's neat, sloping writing: *I saw* Hamish Macbeth *on TV last night and brushed up my Scottish accent.*

I scribble down my reply and casually pass it to Jeff. *Yer a fiiine upstanding haggis.* He snorts and Ms. Gelder says, "Yes, Jeff, anything you want to share?" I have a hard time stifling my laughter.

After class, Jeff and I head for the lockers together. We laugh and kid around. Okay, so nothing's that hugely funny, but it's so great to be with Jeff. And it's the same old crappy school, with the dented lockers, the smell of sweaty socks and sneakers, but it feels good, so good.

I say, wickedly, "Hey, when you come over this weekend, you can try and pick up an Indian accent. That should really impress my grandmother."

I burst out laughing as Jeff's eyes flicker with alarm.

We pass Lynne, who's fumbling at her locker. I smile widely at her and say hi. She looks surprised, mumbles hi, then drops her eyes.

"What was that about?" asks Jeff.

"I'll tell you some other time."

Hey, I refuse to let Lynne get to me.

Jeff stands around by my locker, and Erin comes up and joins in, as though the three of us have always hung out together. Behind his back, she wiggles her eyebrows at me and grins knowingly before rushing off to band. Jeff and I are practically the last ones out of school.

"I'll call you later, okay?" He squeezes my hand.

The look in his eyes turns my insides to jelly.

I walk on air all the way home.

Mom's car is in the driveway, but not Dad's.

I come down with a thud.

How did they get along today, Naniji and Mom? I mean, Mom's no slouch in the fierce department, either.

I start to laugh. Oh God. Me, from both of them. Double the fierce.

I open the door.

There's a subdued thud coming from the family room. Nina and her horde are really into wannabe alternative bands that everyone else got over last year.

"Tara-My-Stara," calls Mom eagerly. "We're in the kitchen."

Okay. No blood so far.

Mom and Naniji are drinking tea at the table, and Maya's sipping lemonade from a china cup.

"Hello, love," says Mom.

"Hi, Mom; hi, Naniji."

I look anxiously at Naniji.

She smiles at me, her eyes warm. "Hello, Tara, how was school?"

My shoulders unknot. I guess I was a little afraid she'd be embarrassed or reserved after yesterday. "Fine."

I drop a kiss on Maya's cheek and say, "And how was your day, Naniji? What did you do?"

Naniji starts to say something, and so does Mom, and then they both stop.

"After you, Mummyji," says Mom, smoothly.

Naniji says, "Your mummyji came home early, and we went to the Byward Market. It was most beautiful."

Oh God, it's her determined-to-be-pleased voice again.

"Yes," trills Mom, "it was a lovely day, unexpectedly warm for this time of year. We were almost tempted to sit outside with our cappuccinos."

Mom and Naniji over cappuccino! The mind boggles.

They smile earnestly at each other—but somehow it's different from before. They're still awkward, but they're less hostile. I feel a surge of love for them. They'll never really like each other, but they're trying, how they're trying.

Impulsively, I reach out and squeeze their hands, Mom on my right, Naniji on my left.

Naniji smiles gratefully, then winces as Nina's music suddenly cranks up.

Maya runs into the family room, shouting, "Dancing, yaaayyy!"

Mom looks quickly at Naniji, then roars, "Hey, Nina, turn that down."

I grunt, "I'll do it."

I go into the family room, and there are Nina and her friends, bopping away, with Maya at the edge trying to copy their every move.

"Tara, do you have to?" snaps Nina as I turn the music way down.

"Yes, Mom told me. Does it have to be so blaring?"

Nina clicks her tongue and huffs, "Come on, guys, let's go to my room."

She and her friends march upstairs with Maya trailing behind.

I roll my eyes and grin.

The phone's ringing, but before I can get to it, Mom answers.

"Tara, for you," she says, eyebrow slightly arched. "Jeff."

I flush slightly, grab the cordless phone, and head for my room.

I take the stairs two at a time.